"'Tis a genial, festive season, and we love to muse upon graves, and dead bodies, and murders, and blood."

-Jerome K. Jerome, 1891

A Very Frightful Victorian Christmas

Curated by:
Amanda R. Woomer

(A Very Frightful Victorian Christmas)
Copyright © 2021 by (Amanda R. Woomer)

Original Cover Artwork Designed by
Copyright © 2021 by (Emily Wayland)

All rights reserved. No part of this book may be reproduced or transmitted in any form or by any means without written permission from the author.

ISBN 979-8-772-46304-8

Printed in USA by Spook-Eats Publishing

For the ones that love Christmas as much as I love Halloween: Mom, Adam, and Toby.

For Jed, who we miss at the holidays most of all.

And for dad, who tried to answer my question all those years ago…

Other Books from Spook-Eats by Amanda R. Woomer:

A Haunted Atlas of Western New York:
a Spooky Guide to the Strange and Unusual

THE SPIRIT GUIDE:
America's Haunted Breweries, Distilleries, and Wineries

The Ghosts of the Ghostlight Theatre

The Feminine Macabre

Creepy Books for Creepy Kids:
The Cryptid ABC Book
Krampus's Great Big Book of Yuletide Monsters

Contents

Introduction: Gather 'Round the Fire

The Christmas Ghost (1915)
   Anna Alice Chapin 1
An 1899 Recipe for Wassail Punch 15
The Body-Snatcher (1884)
   Robert Louis Stevenson 17
A Strange Christmas Game (1868)
   J.H. Riddell 47
An 1845 Recipe for Mock Turtle Soup 59
The Mistletoe Bough (c.1830)
   Thomas Haynes Bayly 62
The Old Nurse's Story (1852)
   Elizabeth Gaskell 64
An 1827 Recipe for Mince Pies 98
The Doll's Ghost (1894)
   F. Marion Crawford 101
The Lover's Farewell (1859)
   Catherine Crowe 123
An 1896 Recipe for Oyster Stew 128
Between the Lights (1912)
   E.F. Benson 130
The Ghost's Summons (1868)
   Ada Buisson 145
An 1862 Recipe for Hot Brandy and Rum Punch 157
Horror: A True Tale (1861)
   John Berwick Harwood 158
Was It an Illusion? A Parson's Story (1881)
   Amelia B. Edwards 201

An 1896 Recipe for Figgy Pudding 233
The Kit-Bag (1901)
    Algernon Blackwood 236
Meet the Authors...257

Gather 'Round the Fire

When I was a young girl, I remember coming out of an antique store with my family to the sound of Andy Williams' voice singing *It's the Most Wonderful Time of the Year* on the radio. The song had always bothered me, and I finally decided to bring the issue up.

"Dad?" I asked. "Why does he say 'scary ghost stories?' It's Christmas, not Halloween."

My dad paused for a moment and tried to come up with an answer. "Think of *A Christmas Carol*," he finally said. "That's a scary ghost story."

He had made up the answer on the spot (as most parents do at times), but he didn't realize he was 100% correct.

A Christmas Carol isn't just one of the most famous Christmas stories, it's also one of the most famous ghost stories. But it certainly isn't the only one. In fact, other beloved writers such as Robert Louis Stevenson, J.M. Barrie, and even Edgar Allan Poe all wrote ghost stories published and told around Christmas and New Year. Everyone from the world's favorite writers to anonymous authors featured in periodicals to even just friends trying to spook each other around the fireplace all participated in the tradition of telling ghost stories on Christmas Eve in the 19th and early 20th Centuries.

The idea of the holidays being a dark and frightening time was not a concept specific to the Victorian-Era. For centuries, stories were told during the long, dark nights as the snow fell outside and the fire burned low—stories that brought us Krampus, the Yule Cat, the Tomtar, and the Kallikantzaros. Before the modern luxuries of electricity, heat, indoor plumbing, and grocery stores, the winter months were a terrifying and challenging time. There was no guarantee that you would survive into the spring. And so, winter was the most frightful time of year (no matter what Andy Williams says). Telling ghost stories transformed from a folk custom of the lower class to a festive pastime at Christmas parties spanning social classes and was locked into the English holiday tradition after Charles Dickens published *A Christmas Carol* in 1843.

Of course, telling ghost stories at Christmas time was not embraced by everyone. The Puritans looked down at the superstitious (and, according to them, evil) custom, leaving behind the tradition as they traveled to the new world. Washington Irving (author of *The Legend of Sleepy Hollow*) attempted to bring the custom over to the United States in the early 19th Century. However, it still struggled to take off, which wasn't helped when Irish and Scottish immigrants arrived in America and brought with them Samhain… Halloween.

Over the last century, Halloween has become the nightmarish holiday (especially in America), filled with ghosts and goblins, while Christmas has been transformed into a time of merriment, mandated joy, and extreme commercialization. And yet, despite the bright lights, tinsel, and colorful wrapping paper, there seems to be a return to the old way of doing things. People have struggled with the pressures of gift-giving and appearing grateful and blessed at the holidays to the point where many dread the holiday season. Some even despise it. With the pressure for the perfect Christmas party, the drive to find that sought-after gift, and the toxic consumer industry that has appeared over the last fifty years, perhaps now is the perfect time to resurrect Dickens' Christmas ghost stories.

Many of these ghost stories (most prominent in *A*

Christmas Carol) remind us that generosity, forgiveness, and kindness unify us and are the true gifts we can give one another. Life can be difficult, so why not lessen each other's burdens before our time is up?

It's also true among families grieving the loss of loved ones that "the veil" seems to be just as thin (if not thinner) during the holidays than at Halloween. Many times, people have paranormal encounters with deceased friends and family during the winter months. Even throughout the Victorian age, many of the stories shared on Christmas Eve were actual ghostly encounters people experienced and not just fictional fantasies. It would seem grief, like ghost stories, transcends time.

I suppose, in the end, we're all fated to become ghost stories told around a fire on Christmas Eve… just make sure your story is worth listening to. And in the meantime, I hope this book will help you create memories with friends and family and that these stories might entertain you during the holidays just as they did over one-hundred years ago.

A Very Frightful Victorian Christmas

Curated by:
Amanda R. Woomer

The Christmas Ghost
By: Anna Alice Chapin
1915

"And it's going to be a real Christmas Eve party—old fashioned, you know, with an open fire, and ghost stories, and punch with baked apples in it, and—"

"And a flash-light!"

"Who told you? A flash-light... How beastly!"

"No... What fun! What a lovely idea! Was it one of Candace's?"

"I think it was. She wanted a record of the evening, and we are all to have copies of the pictures to keep as souvenirs."

They were all merry and chattered like young birds, all except Myra Randall. She smiled and was cheerful enough in a way, but she had never quite seemed carefree since the breaking of her engagement to Max Atwood two years before.

Candace Jewett, the young hostess tonight, had been trying for months to bring the two together again and had gone so far as to include them both in her Christmas Eve party, but neither Max nor Myra was happy about it. They had been cool and calm and polite with each other, but nothing more.

Candace was disappointed enough to cry. Pulling Myra into a corner while the others were laughing and discussing the best games for twelve people, she wrapped her friend in a hug.

"Myra," she began with that ghost of a stammer which her many admirers found so irresistible, "why don't you make up with Max? He's such a darling."

Myra was tall and dainty, with gray eyes and a vast amount of smooth, red-brown hair. She was a girl who went hunting a great deal and looked it. She was equally perfect in a riding habit and in full evening dress.

She raised her brow with a slightly mocking expression.

"Sorry, my dear," she said. "But I can't do that, even to oblige you. Max is attractive…"

She looked down the room and through the door to the young man who was joking and flirting with Letty Lovell.

They were preparing some mysterious game, weaving string around every conceivable object.

"He is attractive," Myra repeated. "But frankly, Candy, I can't marry a man who has no more heart than… than… than a crocodile."

"Myra Randall!" Candace gasped. "How dare you compare our Max to a c-crocodile? He has the warmest, kindest, nicest, understandingest heart in the world!"

"Candace," Myra said, looking straight in front of her. Candace could see her slender, strong hands clenched hard at her sides. "Beatrix loved Max, and he loved her. And yet, within one year of her death, he can joke and play at love again like that."

Candace nearly fell into the fire in surprise. Myra was the most unexpected person.

"Beatrix?" she repeated almost stupidly. "Beatrix! Who died last Christmas time?"

"Yes," Myra said. "My cousin, Beatrix. Did you ever suspect it? They cared for each other… that was why I broke off the engagement."

"But… Did he… Did she tell you? I don't see how—"

"I heard Beatrix telephone him from here that Christmas Eve two years ago when we were all together. Do you remember?"

"Of course! Our first house party since we were all grown up and out in society."

"Well, you know Max had sent word he couldn't get out until Christmas Day. On the afternoon on the day before Christmas, I was curled up there," Myra pointed to the little room opening out of the big library where they all were, "dozing over a book. And," she laughed bitterly, "thinking of Max. You see, I adored him then.

"I heard a little rustle, and Beatrix passed the half-open door and went to the telephone in the hall. She did not see me, and it never occurred to me to let her know I was there until I heard her say, 'Oh, Max, my darling! Is it you? Yes, they're all upstairs dressing. No, there's no chance of her overhearing.' Of course, I can't repeat it all."

Myra's color faded from her face at the memory, but she went steadily on.

"They agreed to meet in London that evening for the last time. They had agreed to give each other up, you see. Do you remember that Beatrix was called to town suddenly that evening?"

"To see her aunt who was ill. Yes."

"And came back the next day on the same train with Max?"

Candace nodded, speechless.

"Well," Myra said, "that was all—and then I broke the engagement."

"Did you ever tell them?"

"No. I tried to save their feelings."

Myra laughed and shrugged her shoulders.

"You see," she added simply, "I was fond of them both. So I was quite sorry when it never came to anything between them despite my setting Max free. I suppose they must have quarreled. And a year later, she was dead."

"And you still wear mourning for her?" Candace shook her head.

"Why not?" said Myra in faint surprise, looking down at her black dinner dress. "She was my first cousin, and I loved her dearly. Beatrix was such a splendid, vital creature, with such will and poise. And to think that she is now dead!"

Candace left her silently and went across to where Letty and Sibyl were talking in low voices.

"You seem very solemn, girls!" she said, trying to speak lightly.

"Sib was saying how Beatrix would have loved it tonight," Letty said.

Candace shifted, suddenly uncomfortable.

"Beatrix seems to be in the air tonight!" she said, almost impatiently.

"Well," Sibyl said, "she said she would be, you know."

"What on earth do you mean?" exclaimed Letty.

"Why, don't you remember how she used to laugh and say, 'If I die first, girls, I'll come back and haunt you! I'll never be quiet in my grave.'"

"We were just an even dozen then, counting Beatrix, at our party two years ago," Letty sighed. "We're only eleven now, aren't we?"

"No, still twelve," Candace said. "My kid brother, Jack, is old enough now to join us. And with Gracie's brother, Jimmy, Max and Rudolph, the two Graves boys, and Colin Clay, we're an even dozen still. But I didn't want to ask an extra girl," she added, hesitatingly. "Somehow, on Beatrix's behalf, I thought I'd let Jack be with twelfth."

She went off to oversee the arrival of the great bowl of steaming punch in which the baked apples floated in the true old English style.

Corby Grange had been given over to the young people that Christmas Eve. Candace's father had slipped away to the study at the back of the house so that her guests might be at liberty to make merry until dawn if they liked.

And, of course, they took advantage of it to romp and laugh and pretend they were school children again. They played games, sang carols, and told fortunes. Then, finally, Candace suggested playing "Oracles."

No one knew anything about it.

"You play it like this," she explained. "Each of us writes a question and folds it up and writes a number on the inside. Then everyone draws from a hat a slip of blank paper with a number written on it and writes an answer to an imaginary question. Just any foolish thing you like: 'Yes,' or 'Not at all,' or 'They are better with onions.' You could even put a mysterious prophecy or a sentimental message—anything you like! Then you put them into a hat or bowl and take them up to the Oracle. And then people go up one by one and read their number, and the Oracle hands them the corresponding answer, and they have to read aloud the question and answer. It's awfully funny sometimes!"

It was an absurd game, of course, but young people can get fun out of anything at Christmas time. So, they appointed Jimmy Markwell the Oracle and settled down to play the game.

After they had written all the papers, they turned the answers over to Jimmy, who sat in a mysterious corner behind a fire screen.

They put out all the lights except one ghostly candle. Then one by one, they went up and received their messages from Fate. Some of the combinations of the questions and answers made no sense, and they had one or two good laughs before it came to Myra Randall's turn.

She walked the length of the dark room, almost invisible in her somber gown.

"Number eleven," she said very quietly.

She now felt that the question she had written had been a foolish one. Not just foolish—indiscreet. She dreaded having to read it out loud.

The Oracle handed over a slip. She approached the one candle. It flickered so that she could hardly see to read.

"'Question: Should you believe your own eyes and ears when you do not want to?'"

"Hold on! There's an awful draft in here," Max interrupted. "I'll draw the curtain."

Myra put her hand to her throat and went on. "'Answer: The eyes and ears of the living are dulled by earth.'" She stopped short, appalled. How could such an answer have come by chance? Someone must have read her question before writing the answer.

"By Jove!" Rudolph said, clearly uncomfortable.

"There's no fun if it comes out as well as that! Who wrote it anyway—the answer, I mean? Well, don't all speak at once!"

No one spoke.

The candle had stopped flickering and now was burning with a clear, steady light. In its rather ghostly rays, the faces of twelve friends looked pale and unnatural.

Candace was the first to speak.

"I… I don't think this has turned out to be a very funny game," she said nervously. "Let's try something more amusing."

"Yes!" said Rudolph. "Let's tell ghost stories or go and visit the graveyard, or do something really lively and cheerful."

"Next!" called the Oracle. "We might as well finish, Candy. You're the only one left."

"Twelve," stammered Candy.

Her question was about making an offer of marriage. The answer—easily traceable to Sibyl Lee—was concerned with manners. It was not a particularly amusing combination, but they all laughed hysterically. It was much better than Myra's depressing coincidence.

"So that's your stupid game!" said Sibyl scornfully. "Well, I don't think much of that—"

"Number thirteen," someone said in the darkness.

They all jumped.

"Who on earth said that?" demanded the Oracle.

"Somebody is fooling," Max said at once. "The game is over… There are only twelve of us here!"

"But there's a paper here. Two papers here!" protested the Oracle.

"I suppose it's Rudolph," Candace said. "He's always playing jokes."

She spoke as if Rudolph was not sitting in the room.

"I swear I didn't," he protested.

"Read them out loud, Jimmy," Max said.

"It's too dark," said the Oracle. "I can't see to read over here. Bring me that candle."

The candle was misbehaving again, but in a moment, it stopped and burned clearly once more. Max carried it across the room and held it while Jimmy read out slowly and with many pauses:

"'Number thirteen. Question: What was Beatrix doing on Christmas Eve two years ago?'"

"Oh, Jimmy, that is too much!" Candace gasped, shocked. "Beatrix is dead. No one should drag her name into this nonsense."

"I can't help it!" the Oracle cried. "That's what's on the paper. Someone's written it!"

"Then someone has very bad taste!" Sibyl declared.

"Do you want to hear the answer?" Jimmy asked.

Candace hesitated, but to everyone's surprise, Max spoke. "Yes, please," he said quietly. "Let's have the answer."

And Jimmy read:

"'Number thirteen. Answer: On Christmas Eve, one year before she died, Beatrix went to the telephone at Corby Grange and pretended to call up Max. She knew that Myra was in the next room, and she let her think that she was exchanging words of love with the man Myra was engaged to.

"'She made believe she was agreeing to an appointment in town that evening and Myra saw her leave for the evening train. She and Max came to Corby Grange together the next day, and Myra broke the engagement. Myra did not know that Beatrix had not spoken to Max for weeks until she met him on the train that morning—'

"I can hardly read this," Jimmy said. "It's so scrawly and queer—as if it had been written in a hurry.

"'—nor that the receiver…' I think it's receiver. '—nor that the receiver had never been taken off the hook.'"

There was a dead silence in the room when suddenly, without warning, the candle went out.

Candace screamed. Sibyl clung to Rudolph. Grace and Letty Lovell had both burst into tears. Myra did not cry, but she shook from head to foot with a strange excitement that was not entirely terror. Someone touched her hand softly in the darkness. Instinctively, she knew it was Max.

"It's all right," he said nervously in her ear. "They'll find a match in a minute. Just an absurd, rather rotten joke of someone's."

"A joke?" Myra gasped. "Oh Max, is it true what the thirteenth paper said?"

"I suppose so," he said gently. "I never received a telephone message from Beatrix in my life."

"Max!" she whispered, and he had time to draw her near him and kiss her before a rather bright match flared up.

"See here," Rudolph said as he lit, not the candle, but the gas lamp. "I've had enough of this Oracle business."

"It was ghostly," said Candace, wiping a tear from her cheek. "Who would have written those things?"

"I suggest," said Jimmy earnestly, "that we never try to find out."

A knock sounded at the door.

"Are they ready for the photograph?"

They welcomed the diversion, but twelve rather solemn young faces looked at the man with the camera.

"One of you moved, didn't you, during the flash?" the photographer asked.

"I don't think so," someone replied.

"But just as I touched off the flash, I thought I saw a pale young woman in a white dress sitting next to the tall gentleman. As you see, she is not there now."

Candace jumped back.

"No lady here tonight is wearing a white dress," she said as she caught her breath.

"Oh, my mistake!" murmured the mystified photographer. "It—it might have been a window shade... or a curtain."

"Yes, of course," Candace agreed hastily.

The pictures were never sent around as souvenirs. Instead, the plate was discovered years later. For in the group in the photograph, there was a thirteenth person, and the face was the face of Beatrix, who had been dead a year.

Wassail Punch

Inspired by an 1899 Recipe

Ingredients:
4 apples, cut in half and cored
1 cup of brown sugar
4 cloves
½ gallon of apple cider
3 tbsp of brandy
1/3 cup of sugar
1 tsp of ground ginger
1 sachet of mulling spices
2 cinnamon sticks
3 orange slices
3 lemon slices
Nutmeg

Directions:
1. Preheat the oven to 350°F.
2. Slice the apples in half and cut out the core. Fill the hole with brown sugar. Bake for approximately 40 minutes.
3. Pour the cider and brandy into a thick-bottomed saucepan and heat gently over low heat. Do not boil. Add the sugar and ground ginger.
4. Place the mulling spices and cinnamon sticks into the pan. Allow to heat up for approximately 25 minutes. Remove the sachet.

5. Float the baked apples, orange slices, and lemon slices in the punch.
6. Optional: Transfer to a heat-safe punch bowl.
7. Top with fresh ground nutmeg.

Wassail is both a hot mulled beverage and the act of going door to door, singing songs in exchange for charity (be it money, gifts, food, or drink). Wassail dates back to the 12th Century, first appearing in text in 1140.

Wassail evolved over the years. Early forms included mead with crab apples floating in it. Modern versions start with a base of apple cider, fruit juice, wine, or ale. Many times, apples and oranges are added along with brandy or sherry (to help keep you warm, of course!), as well as spices such as cinnamon, nutmeg, and ginger.

Wassail recipes didn't just vary from region to region over the centuries but from family to family as well. This 1899 recipe is similar to the punch with baked apples Candace had at her party with Myra, Max, and the others.

The Body-Snatcher
By: Robert Louis Stevenson
1884

Every night throughout the year, four of us sat in the small parlor of The George at Debenham—the Undertaker, the Landlord, Fettes, and myself. Sometimes there would be more, but blow high, blow low, come rain or snow or frost, we four would always be planted in our usual armchairs.

Fettes was an old drunken Scotsman, a man of education and property. He had come to Debenham years ago, while still young, and by simply sticking around, had grown to be an adopted townsman. His blue cloak was a local antiquity, like the church spire. His place in the parlor at The George, his absence from the church, and his old and disreputable vices were all expected in Debenham. He had some vague radical opinions and some fleeting affairs. He drank rum—five glasses each evening—and spent the majority of his night at The George, sitting in a state of melancholy alcoholic stupor with his half-drunk glass in his right hand. We called him the Doctor, for he was supposed to have some knowledge of medicine and had been known (when in a pinch) to be able to set a fracture or two. But beyond these slight particulars, we had no knowledge of his character or his history.

One dark winter night—it had struck nine sometime before the Landlord joined us—there was a sick man in The George. He had suffered from a stroke on his way to Parliament. The great man's even greater London doctor had been telegraphed to his bedside. It was the first time that such a thing had happened in Debenham (for the railway was newly opened), and we were all excited by the events.

"He's come," the Landlord said after he had filled and lit his pipe.

"Who?" I asked. "The doctor?"

"Indeed."

"What's his name?"

"Dr. Macfarlane," said the Landlord.

Fettes was deep into his third glass of rum, stupidly fuddled and nodding over. He was staring lazily around him, but he seemed to awaken at the mention of the man's name.

"Macfarlane," he whispered to himself before repeating with sudden emotion, "Macfarlane?"

"Yes," the Landlord replied. "That's his name. Dr. Wolfe Macfarlane."

Fettes became instantly sober. His eyes awoke, his voice became clear, loud, and steady. We were all startled by the sudden transformation as if a man had risen from the dead.

"I beg your pardon," he said. "I'm afraid I have not been paying much attention. Who is this Wolfe Macfarlane?" Then, after he heard the Landlord repeat himself, he added, "It cannot be… It cannot be. And yet, I would like to see him face to face."

"Do you know him, Doctor?" the Undertaker asked with a gasp.

"God have mercy! The name is a strange one… Tell me, Landlord, is he old?"

"Well," said the host, "he's not a young man—his hair is white—but he looks younger than you."

"He is older though… years older. But," Fettes added with a slap on the table, "it's the rum you see in my face—rum and sin…"

"If you know this doctor," I ventured to say after a somewhat awful pause, "I gather you don't share the Landlord's good opinion of the man."

Fettes didn't notice me or my question.

"I must see him face to face," he repeated himself.

There was another pause when a door slammed shut upstairs, and the men could hear footsteps on the wooden stairs.

"That's the doctor," cried the Landlord. "Be quick, and you can catch him!"

The George Inn was small. It was barely two steps from the parlor to the door. The wide oak staircase landed in the street, and nothing but a small rug fit between the final step and the threshold. But this little space was brilliantly lit up each evening, not only by the light upon the staircase and the signal-lamp below the sign but by the warm radiance of the bar-room window. The George always brightly advertised itself to passers-by on the street.

Fettes marched steadily to the staircase, and the three of us hung back, watching the two men meet (as Fettes put it) face to face.

Dr. Macfarlane was alert. His white hair set off his pale yet energetic countenance. He was dressed in the finest suit with a great gold watch chain, and studs and spectacles of the same precious metal. He wore a broad-folded tie, white and speckled with lilac, and he carried on his arm a comfortable driving-coat of fur. It was a surprising contrast to see our Doctor—bald, dirty, pimpled, and robed in his old cloak—confront him at the foot of the stairs.

"Macfarlane!" he called out to the man.

The great doctor pulled up short on the fourth step as though the familiarity of his name being called out surprised him.

"Toddy Macfarlane!" Fettes repeated.

The London man nearly staggered. He stared for a moment at the man before him, glanced around him at the bar, and then in a startled whisper, "Fettes? Is that you?"

"Aye." He nodded. "It's me. Did you think I was dead too? Apparently, we can't escape each other."

"Hush!" the doctor exclaimed. "I didn't recognize you at first. I'm happy to see you, but for now, it must be 'How do you do?' and also 'Goodbye!' for my cab is waiting for me. Leave me your address, and I will call on you early tomorrow. I must do something for you, Fettes… for auld lang syne, as we used to sing."

"Money?" Fettes scoffed. "Money from you? The money that you gave me is still lying where I cast it in the rain."

Dr. Macfarlane had talked himself into some kind of superiority and confidence, but this sudden and unexpected refusal cast him back into his confusion.

A horrible, ugly look came and went across his otherwise cheerful face. "My dear fellow," he said, "have it as you wish. I don't want to offend you. Let me leave you my address—"

"I don't want it. I do not wish to know the roof that shelters you," Fettes interrupted. "I heard your name, and I feared it might be you. I wished to know if there was a God… now I know there isn't one. Begone!"

He stood in the middle of the rug at the base of stairs, and the great London physician, in order to escape, would be forced to step to one side. It was plain that he hesitated at the thought of this humiliation. Yet, as clean as he was, there was a dangerous look in his eyes, hiding behind his spectacles. As he hesitated, he became aware of his driver peering in from the street at this unusual scene and noticed our little group from the parlor, huddled by the corner of the bar.

The presence of so many witnesses made the decision for him, and he fled. Brushing against the wainscot, he leaped for the door, but not before Fettes grabbed his arm and whispered, "Have you seen it again?"

The wealthy London doctor cried out loud with a sharp cry. He pushed Fettes back and fled out of the door like a thief with his hands over his head. Before anyone could act, the cab was gone, rattling toward the station.

The scene was over like a dream, but the dream had left traces of its passage. The following day, the servant found the fine gold spectacles broken on the threshold, and that very night we were all standing breathless by the bar-room window, and Fettes at our side, sober, pale, and resolute.

"God, protect us, Mr. Fettes!" said the Landlord, coming to his senses. "What in the world was all that?"

Fettes turned toward us, looking into each of our faces. "Speak of this to no one," he warned us. "That man, Macfarlane, is not safe. Many men have crossed his path and regretted it only when it was too late."

And then, without so much as finishing his third glass (much less the other two), he bade us goodnight and disappeared into the black night.

The three of us returned to our places in the parlor, with the big red fire and four clear candles, and as we thought back to the events that had passed, the initial chill of our surprise soon changed into curiosity. We sat long—it was the latest session I have known in the old George. Each of us, before we parted, had our own theory that we were determined to prove.

I should not boast, but I believe I was better at discovering the story—far better than my fellows at The George. And perhaps I am the only man who can narrate to you the following foul and unnatural events.

In his young days, Fettes studied medicine in Edinburgh. He was talented—he could pick up what he heard and master it quickly. He rarely worked at home but was civil, attentive, and intelligent in the presence of his masters. They soon recognized him as a lad who listened closely and remembered well. As strange as it may have been for me to imagine, he was well-favored, handsome, and lucky in those days.

There was, at this time, an anatomy teacher whom I shall simply call Dr. K (but I'm sure you know who he is). Dr. K snuck through the streets of Edinburgh in disguise while the mob applauded at the execution of Burke, calling for the blood of his employer. But Dr. K was a master of disguise and was well-liked by his students... including Fettes. By his second year in school, he was an assistant in Dr. K's class.

Fettes was responsible for the operating theatre and the lecture room. He had to answer for the cleanliness of the premises and the behavior of the other students. It was also his duty to supply, receive, and divide the various subjects. And it was with these subjects that Fettes worked directly with Dr. K, living not only on the same street as the doctor but in the same building. It was here, after a night of drinking—his hands still trembling and his eyes still misty and confused—that he would be called out of bed in the black hours before the winter dawn by the unclean and desperate men who supplied the table. He would open the door to these men—infamous throughout the land. He would help them with their tragic burden, pay them their wicked price, and remain alone once they were gone, with the unfriendly relics of humanity. After, he would crawl back into bed and snatch another hour or two of slumber to repair himself from the abuses of the night and refresh himself for the day.

Few lads could be as unfeeling to the impressions of a life having just passed the threshold from this life into the next. His mind was shut off. He couldn't afford to be interested in the fate and fortunes of anyone. He was desperate for the admiration from his masters and fellow pupils, and he had no desire to fail. And so, he made it his mission to gain distinction in his studies and each day proved himself useful to his employer, Dr. K.

The supply of subjects was a continual burden to him as well as his master. In that large class, the raw material of the anatomists was always running out, and the business necessary to restock their supply was not only unpleasant but dangerous to anyone involved.

It was Dr. K's policy not to ask questions. "They bring the body, and we pay the price," he used to say. "Quid pro quo." He would always repeat himself to his assistants. "Ask no questions, for conscience's sake."

There was no suspicion that the crime of murder provided the subjects. Had that idea been brought up to Fettes, he would have recoiled in horror. But the lightness in Dr. K's speech about so grave a matter was, in itself, an offense against all things good and surely tempted the men he worked with. Fettes, for instance, had often thought to himself that the bodies always seemed so fresh. He had also noticed how dastardly the ruffians looked as they stood on his doorstep each night before dawn. But he couldn't afford to let his thoughts venture too far into the dark. He understood his duty: to take what was brought, pay the price, and avert the eyes from any evidence of crime.

One November morning, this policy of silence was put to the test. He had been awake all night with a toothache—pacing his room like a caged beast or throwing himself in a fury onto his bed—and had at last fallen into an uneasy slumber when a loud bang on the door awoke him.

The moon shone bright, and it was bitter cold, windy, and frosty. The town had not yet awakened, but there was a stir in the air. The ghoulish men had come later than usual, and they seemed more than usually eager to be gone.

Fettes, desperate to go back to sleep, lit the stairs. He heard their grumbling voices through a dreamy fog. He leaned against the wall, dozing, as they pulled the subject from their sack. Then, shaking himself awake to find the men their money, his eyes glanced at the dead face. Startled, he took two steps forward with the candle raised.

"God Almighty!" he cried. "That is Jane Galbraith!"

The men didn't say a word. Instead, they simply shuffled toward the door.

"I know her!" he continued, his voice trembling. "She was alive and hearty yesterday. She can't be dead. It's impossible you got this body fairly."

"Sir, you must be mistaken," one of the men said.

But the other man looked darkly into Fettes' eyes and demanded the money on the spot.

It was impossible to ignore the man's silent threat. The lad's heart failed him. He stammered for excuses, counted out the sum, and saw his wicked visitors depart. No sooner were they gone than he ran to the body to confirm his doubts. By a dozen unquestionable marks, he identified the girl he had only spoken with the day before. He saw, with horror, marks upon her body that were signs of violence. He panicked and hid away in his room. There, he reflected over the discovery he had made—considered the meaning of Dr. K's instructions and the danger he was now in, Fettes decided to ask his fellow class assistant for advice.

This was a young doctor, Wolfe Macfarlane, a favorite among all the students—he was clever, handsome, and unscrupulous. He had traveled and studied abroad. His manners were agreeable, even if they were a bit forward. He was gifted at riding, skating, and golf, dressed with style, and was at ease in the operating theatre. With Fettes, he was friendly—their positions as class assistants called for them to work closely together. In fact, when subjects were scarce, the pair would drive into the country, visit and desecrate some lonely graveyard, and return before dawn with their booty.

On that particular morning, Macfarlane arrived somewhat earlier than usual. Fettes heard him and met him on the stairs. He told his classmate his story and showed him his cause for alarm. Macfarlane studied the marks on her body.

"Yes," he said with a nod. "It does look suspicious."

"What should we do?" Fettes asked.

"Do?" Macfarlane repeated the question. "Do you want to do anything? Least said soonest mended, I say."

"Someone else might recognize her," Fettes objected. "She was as well-known as the Castle Rock."

"Let's hope not," Macfarlane said. "And if anybody does, you didn't. The fact is, this has been going on for a long time. But don't stir up trouble—you'll get K in an unholy mess, and I'm sure you'll get dragged into it too… as will I. What would we say in a witness box? There's no doubt that all of our subjects have been murdered."

"Macfarlane!" Fettes cried out.

"Come now," he sneered. "As if you haven't suspected it yourself."

"Suspecting is one thing…"

"And proof is another. I'm as sorry as you are about Miss Galbraith," he sighed, tapping the body with his cane. "The next best thing to do is not recognize her. I certainly don't," he added coldly. "I won't tell you what you should do, but I think a man of the world would do as I do. And I might add: I think that is what Dr. K would expect of both of us. He chose us to be his two assistants for a reason."

Fettes agreed to follow Macfarlane's example. The body of the unfortunate girl was dissected, and no one appeared to recognize her.

One afternoon, when his day's work was over, Fettes dropped into a popular tavern and found Macfarlane sitting with a stranger. It was a small man, very pale with coal-black eyes. His features suggested intellect, but his manners were coarse, vulgar, and stupid. However, he seemed to hold a remarkable control over Macfarlane—barking orders and then mocking the young doctor's hesitations. This offensive person took a fancy to Fettes on the spot, offered him drinks, and offered him compliments about the future of his career. If a small portion of what he admitted was true, he was a most wicked man, indeed, and the young boy's vanity was tickled by the attention of a man so experienced in the ways of the world.

"I'm a pretty bad fellow, myself," the stranger remarked. "But Macfarlane is the boy—Toddy Macfarlane, I call him. Toddy, order your friend another drink. Toddy hates me, you see," he laughed.

"Don't call me that," Macfarlane growled.

"Listen to him! Do you ever watch the young boys play with knives? Well, Toddy would like to do that all over my body," the stranger remarked.

"We medicals have a much better way than that," Fettes said. "When we dislike a dead friend, we dissect him."

Macfarlane looked up sharply at Fettes as if the thought had already crossed his mind.

The afternoon passed. Gray—that was the stranger's name—invited Fettes to join them for dinner, ordered a feast so sumptuous that the tavern was thrown into a commotion, and when all was done, he commanded Macfarlane to pay the bill.

It was late before they separated, and the man, Gray, was clearly drunk. Sobered by his fury, Macfarlane was still raging about the money he had been forced to squander and the insults he had been forced to swallow. Fettes, with various liquors singing in his head, stumbled home.

Next day, Macfarlane was absent from the class, and Fettes smiled to himself as he imagined the poor lad still taking the intolerable Gray from tavern to tavern. As soon as class was over, Fettes hopped from place to place, searching for last night's companions. He couldn't find them anywhere, so he returned to his rooms, went to bed early, and slept soundly.

At four in the morning, he was awakened by a familiar knock. Descending the stairs to the door, he was shocked to find Macfarlane with his carriage—and in that carriage was a long and ghastly sack he knew so well.

"You went out alone?" Fettes couldn't hide the shock from his voice. "How did you manage?"

But Macfarlane silenced him. When they got the body upstairs and laid it on the table, Macfarlane turned to leave. He paused and seemed to hesitate for a moment before turning to Fettes and whispering, "You had better look at the face. You had better."

Fettes just stared at him in wonder. "Where did you get it? How... and when?"

"Look at the face," was the only answer.

Fettes staggered. His mind was filled with doubts and fears. He looked from the young doctor to the body and then back again. At last, with a start, he did as he was told. He knew what he was going to see, and yet the shock was still just as cruel. To see—rigid in death and naked—the man whom he had left well-dressed and full of meat and sin upon the threshold of the tavern awoke some of the terrors of the conscience buried deep in Fettes.

Hodie Mihi Cras Tibi... Today me, tomorrow you. The thought echoed through his soul—knowing that one of the two men he knew from yesterday had come to lie upon these icy tables. Yet these were only secondary thoughts, for his true concern was for Wolfe.

Afraid to challenge his friend and comrade, he could barely look Macfarlane in the face. Luckily it was Macfarlane, himself, who spoke first. He came up quietly behind and laid his hand gently but firmly on his friend's shoulder.

"Richardson may have the head."

Now Richardson was a student who had long been desperate to dissect that portion of the human subject.

When there was no answer, the murderer added, "Talking of business, you must pay me. Your ledger must line up."

Fettes, at last, found a voice... a ghost of his own. "Pay you?" he cried. "Pay you for that?"

"Why yes, of course. You must," Macfarlane laughed. "I won't give it to you for nothing, and you wouldn't dare take it for nothing. It will be a compromise for both of us. This is another case like Jane Galbraith's. The more things that go wrong, the more we must act as if things are all right. Where does old K keep the money?"

"There," Fettes answered hoarsely, pointing to a cupboard in the corner.

"Give me the key," Macfarlane said calmly, holding out his hand.

There was a moment's hesitation, and the die was cast. Macfarlane could not suppress a nervous twitch—the telltale sign of immense relief—as he felt the key between his fingers. He opened the cupboard, brought out the pen, ink, and a book as well as the sum suitable for such an occasion.

"Now look here," he said, "the payment has been made—proof of your good faith. Enter the payment in your book."

The next few seconds were agony for Fettes. He tried to balance the multitude of terrors he felt, but it was the most immediate that triumphed. Any future difficulty was welcome if he could avoid a quarrel with Macfarlane. He leaned over the book and entered the date, nature, and amount of the transaction with a steady hand.

"And now," Macfarlane said, "it's only fair that you pocket some of the profit. I've had my share already," he handed the money to his friend. "When a man of the world falls into a bit of luck and has a few extra shillings in his pocket, he's to share. Now no purchasing expensive class books, no squaring off old debts, and don't lend it to anyone else."

"Macfarlane," Fettes began, his voice still hoarse. "I have put my neck out to oblige you—"

"Oblige me?" Wolfe cried. "Oh, come on! Suppose I get into trouble, where will you be? This little matter clearly flows from the first. Mr. Gray is simply the continuation of Miss Galbraith. You can't begin and then stop. If you begin, you must keep beginning. No rest for the wicked."

A horrible sense of darkness and treachery seized hold upon the soul of Fettes.

"My God!" he cried. "What have I done? And when did I begin? To be made class assistant—where's the harm in that? William Service wanted the position… Service might have gotten it. Would *he* have been where I am now?"

"My dear fellow," Macfarlane said, "what a boy you are! What harm has come to you? What harm can come to you if you hold your tongue? Do you even know what this life is? There are two groups—the lions and the lambs. If you're a lamb, you'll come to lie upon these tables like Gray and Jane Galbraith. If you're a lion, you'll live and drive a horse like me, like K, like all the world with any wit or courage. You've staggered, but you're clever and plucky. I like you, and K likes you. You were born to lead the hunt. I'll tell you, in my experience, three days from now, you'll laugh at all this."

And with that, Macfarlane drove up the road to get under cover before the sun rose. Fettes was left alone with his regrets. He saw the danger he was now in, and he was no more than Macfarlane's helpless accomplice. He would have given the world to have been a little braver at the time, but it did not occur to him that he might still be brave. The secret of Jane Galbraith and the cursed entry in the ledger silenced him.

Hours passed. Class began to arrive, and the pieces of Gray were handed out to one and to another, each received without remark. Richardson was thrilled to have the head, and before the bell rang, Fettes trembled with excitement at the idea that they had gotten away with it… again.

For two days, Fettes continued to watch with increasing joy and relief.

On the third day, Macfarlane made an appearance. He had been ill, he said, but he made up for lost time by the energy he directed the students. To Richardson in particular, he extended the most valuable assistance and advice. In turn, Richardson, encouraged by Macfarlane's praise, burned high with ambition.

Before the week was out, Macfarlane's prophecy had been fulfilled. Fettes had outlived his terrors and had nearly forgotten them. He had managed to fabricate a story so detailed that he could look back on these events with an unhealthy pride.

Of his accomplice, he saw very little. Of course, they met in class and received their orders from Dr. K, but it was clear that Macfarlane avoided any reference to their shared secret. Even when Fettes whispered to him that he had decided to join the lions and turned his back on the lambs, Macfarlane smiled at him and signed for him to be quiet.

At length, an occasion arose which threw the pair together. Dr. K was again short on subjects—pupils were eager, and it was a teacher's responsibility to always be prepared. At the same time, there was news of a burial in the rustic graveyard of Glencorse. Time has done little to change the place—it stood then as it does now, upon a crossroad, far from human habitation, and buried deep in the shadow of six cedar trees. The cries of the sheep on the neighboring hills, the streams on each side (one singing among the pebbles and the other dripping from pond to pond), the stir of the wind blowing through the flowering chestnuts, and a bell chiming once every seven days were the only sounds that disturbed the silence around the rural church.

The Resurrection Man—to use a nickname of the period—was not to be deterred by the sanctities of any church. On the contrary, it was part of his trade to despise and desecrate the scrolls and trumpets of old tombs, the paths worn by feet of worshippers and mourners, and the offerings and the inscriptions of bereaved affection. To rustic neighborhoods, where love is more tenacious and where the bond of blood or fellowship unites the entire society of a parish, the body-snatcher—repelled by natural respect—was attracted to the ease and safety of the task.

To bodies that had been laid in the earth, with joyful expectation of a far different awakening, there came that hasty, lamp-lit, terrible resurrection of the spade. The coffin was forced open, the wax cloth torn, and the bodies were stuffed into a sack before being rattled for hours on moonless byways, exposed to endless indignities before a class of gaping boys.

As two vultures may swoop upon a dying lamb, Fettes and Macfarlane were to be let loose upon a grave in that green and quiet resting place. The wife of a farmer, a woman who had lived for sixty years, known for good butter and godly conversation, was to be ripped from her grave at midnight and carried, dead and naked, to that far away city that she had always honored with her Sunday best.

Late one afternoon, the pair set off, wrapped in cloaks and prepared with a bottle to keep them warm. It rained without stopping—a cold, dense rain. Now and again, there was a gust of wind, but the rain continued to fall. Even with the bottle, it was a sad and silent drive as far as Penicuik, where they stopped to rest.

They stopped to hide their ghastly tools in a nearby bush not far from the churchyard before they entered the Fisher's Tryst. They toasted as they sat before the kitchen fire and varied their nips of whiskey with a glass of ale.

That night, the two young doctors in a private room sat down to the best dinner and the best wine the house could offer them. The lights, the fire, the beating rain upon the window, the cold and heartless work that lay before them added zest to their enjoyment of the meal. With every glass, their friendliness increased. Soon, Macfarlane handed a little pile of gold to his companion.

"For your troubles," he simply said.

Fettes pocketed the money. "I was an ass until I knew you. You and K will make a man of me yet."

"Of course we will," Macfarlane applauded. "I'll tell you: it took a man to back me up the other morning. There are some big, brawling, forty-year-old cowards who would have turned sick at the sight of the damned thing. But not you... you kept your head."

"And why not?" Fettes complimented himself. "It was not my affair. There was nothing to gain on the one side but an argument with you. And on the other, I could count on your gratitude." He slapped his pocket until the gold pieces rang.

Macfarlane somehow felt a touch of alarm at these unpleasant words. He may have regretted teaching his young companion so well, but he had no time to interrupt, for Fettes continued in his boasting:

"The biggest thing is to not be afraid. Now between you and me, I don't want to hang. But, to be honest, Macfarlane, I was born with contempt for Hell, God, the Devil, right, wrong, sin, crime... those things may frighten boys, but men of the world—like you and me—we despise them." Then, lifting his glass, he added jovially, "Here's to the memory of Gray!"

By that time, it had grown late. The carriage was brought around to the door with both lamps burning bright. The young men paid their bill and started out down the road, announcing that they were bound for Peebles. They drove in that direction until they were clear of the last houses of the town, then extinguishing their lamps, turned around, and followed the road to Glencorse.

There was no sound but that of their own passage and the incessant sound of the pouring rain. It was pitch dark. Here and there, a white gate or a white stone in the wall guided them across the night, but for the most part, it was a slow journey as they picked their way through the darkness to their solemn, isolated destination.

In the sunken woods that traverse the surrounding land of the burying ground, it became necessary to light a match and reilluminate one of the lanterns. And thus, under the dripping trees and surrounded by huge moving shadows, they reached the scene of their unhallowed labors.

The grave in which they stood almost to their shoulders was close to the edge of the plateau of the graveyard. The lantern had been propped up against a tree to better illuminate their work.

They were both experienced in such affairs and powerful with their shovels. They had barely been there for twenty minutes before they were rewarded by a dull rattle on the coffin lid. At the same moment, Macfarlane, having hurt his hand upon a stone, flung it carelessly above his head.

Chance had taken a sure aim with the stone. Then came the clang of broken glass, and night fell upon them. The two men stood still, listening to the sound of the lantern tumbling down the hill and into the stream.

Silence.

They were so close to completing this horrific task that they decided to complete it in the dark. The coffin was exhumed and broken open, the body inserted into the sack and carried between them to the carriage. One man crouched over the body to keep it in its place and the other, taking the horse by the mouth, groped along the stone wall until they reached the wider road by the Fisher's Tryst. Here was a faint, diffused light which they hailed like daylight. With this, they pushed the horse to a good pace and began to rattle merrily along in the direction of town.

They were both soaked to the skin, and now, as the carriage jumped among the deep ruts, their horrible cargo would fall upon one and then the other. Each time they felt the body touch them, they instinctively repelled it with great haste.

Macfarlane made some awful joke about the farmer's wife, but it was hollow as it left his lips and the companions fell into silence once again. Still, their unnatural burden bumped from side to side. Sometimes its head would lay on their shoulders, while other times, the icy cloth would flap about their faces.

A creeping chill began to take hold of Fettes's soul. He peered at the bundle, and it somehow seemed larger than at first. All over the countryside, farm dogs followed after them, barking and growling. Fettes couldn't stop thinking that some unnatural miracle had happened, that some nameless change had befallen the dead body, and that it was in fear of their unholy work that the dogs were howling.

"For God's sake!" Fettes struggled to speak, suddenly overcome with fear. "Let's have a light!"

Apparently, Macfarlane was just as unnerved by the situation as Fettes. Without saying a word, he stopped the horse, passed the reins to his companion, jumped down from the carriage, and lit the remaining lamp. By that time, they had only passed the crossroad to Auchenclinny. The rain still poured with no sign of stopping, and it was nearly impossible to make a light in such a wet, dark world.

When at last the flickering blue flame had been transferred to the wick and began to grow, encircling the carriage in a misty circle of light, the two men were able to see each other and the thing they had with them. The rain had soaked through the sack, pinning the rough material to the outlines of the body underneath—the head was distinct from the feet, the shoulders plainly modeled… something at once spectral and human caught their eyes.

For some time, Macfarlane stood motionless, holding up the lamp. A nameless dread clung to the men like a wet sheet—a meaningless fear, a horror of what could not be, kept popping into his brain.

Another moment passed, and Fettes moved to speak, but his comrade spoke his fears first:

"That is not a woman," Macfarlane said in a hushed voice.

"It was a woman when we put her in," Fettes whispered.

"Hold the lamp," Macfarlane ordered. "I must see her face."

And as Fettes took the lamp, his companion untied the fastenings of the sack and drew down the cover from the head. The light fell very clear upon the dark, well-molded features and smooth-shaven cheeks of a too familiar countenance often beheld in dreams of both these young men.

A wild scream echoed through the night. Each man leaped away from the carriage. The lamp fell, broke, and was extinguished. The horse, terrified by the commotion, bounded and went off toward Edinburgh at a gallop, bearing along with it, the only occupant of the carriage:

The body of the dead and dissected Mr. Gray.

A Strange Christmas Game
By: J.H. Riddell
1868

Thanks to the death of a distant relative, I, John Lester, inherited the Martingdale Estate. When the news arrived, my sister, Clare, and I were the happiest pair in all of England.

You may think it shocking—my sister and I thrilled at our sudden fortune upon the death of our own kinsman, Paul Lester—but we are not hypocrites, nor ones to pretend to mourn a man that was as great a stranger to us as the Prime Minister, the Emperor of Russia, or any other human being so utterly removed from our extremely humble sphere of life. Paul Lester was as distant a relative as one could have—a man whom we had never seen, of whom we had heard very little (and that little being unfavorable), and a man who never helped us despite our years living in poverty.

His loss was most certainly our gain. We had not lost a beloved and honored loved one, but rather, we gained lands, houses, wealth, and respect.

Of course, Martingdale was not much of an estate as far as country properties go. The Lesters who had resided in that region over the course of a few hundred years were anything but prudent. And by the time of Jeremy Lester, the last resident owner of the estate, Martingdale had melted to a mere dot on the map of Bedfordshire.

Along with the estate came a mystery surrounding Jeremy Lester. No one knew what had become of him. On Christmas Eve, long ago, he was sitting in the oak parlor of Martingdale, and before dawn, he had vanished. According to the tale, one Mr. Wharley, a dear friend of Jeremy Lester's, had sat playing cards with him until after midnight, then he took his leave and rode home. After that, no one ever saw Jeremy Lester alive again.

Shortly thereafter, Paul Lester took possession of the house, but he promptly shut up the hall, put in a caretaker, and never returned to his ancestral home.

As years passed, people began to whisper, saying the house was haunted and that Paul Lester had "seen something." The locals insisted that Mr. Jeremy "walked" at Martingdale. They had seen him in the windows over the years, wandering through the empty halls of his once-grand manor.

All of these stories were repeated for our benefit when, forty-one years after the disappearance of Jeremy Lester, Clare and I went down to inspect our inheritance.

Upon our arrival, we met with the caretaker and his wife, who insisted that wild horses, or even wealth beyond her wildest dreams, could not draw her to the red bedroom nor into the oak parlor after dark.

"There are things in those rooms that would make any Christian's hair stand on end. Stamping and swearing. Furniture knocking about. Footsteps up the great staircase, along the corridor, and into the red bedroom. I believe Mr. Paul Lester met him once, and since then, the oak parlor has never been opened."

Upon hearing her ghostly tale, the first thing I did was proceed to the oak parlor, open the shutters, and let the August sun stream into the haunted chamber.

It was an old-fashioned, plainly furnished room, with a large table in the center, a smaller one in the corner near the fireplace, chairs against the walls, and a dusty moth-eaten carpet upon the floor. Paintings hung upon the walls, and the fireplace's brass fender was tarnished and battered. It was a simple, gloomy room that brightened the moment the sun shone through the windows. I knew once we redecorated it, the room would easily transform into a pleasant morning room.

Before we set to work on repairing and redecorating our ancestral home, Clare and I decided to go abroad to take our long-talked-of holiday before the fine weather was gone. A lifetime of struggle made Clare wise, and she declared that we should take our pleasure while we could, for who knew what the next year might bring. So, for several months, we wandered around the continent, loitering in Rouen, visiting galleries in Paris, and befriending our new neighbors in England, the Cronson family.

Claire was less than agreeable with the Cronsons. There was a young woman in England Clare wanted me to think about seriously and possibly marry, but Mr. Cronson had a daughter—Maybel—who was both handsome and attractive. Clare's friend had liked poor John Lester, penniless artist. Miss Cronson had her eyes set on John Lester of

Martingdale and would have turned away from the poor young artist I once was—I can see that plainly enough now. I may have proposed to Maybel if word of family tragedy had not arrived for them. The Cronsons quickly packed up and departed while Clare and I slowly returned to England.

It was the middle of November when we arrived at Martingdale, and we found the place anything but romantic and pleasant. The ghost stories we had laughed at while the sunshine flooded the rooms became more real when we had nothing but blazing fires and wax candles to dispel the gloom. They became even more real when servant after servant left us to seek work elsewhere. Realer still, when the noises of the house grew more frequent—thumping, banging, and clattering.

My dear reader, you are doubtless free from superstitious fancies. You doubt the existence of ghosts and only "wish you could find a haunted house in which to spend the night," which is all very brave and praiseworthy. But wait until you are left in a dreary, desolate, old country mansion, filled with the most unexplainable sounds going on at all hours of the night.

At first, I believed the noises were produced by some thugs intent to keep the house uninhabited, but over time, Clare and I came to the conclusion that the strange activity must be supernatural.

We were practical people, and unlike our predecessors, not having money to live exactly where we liked, we decided to watch and see whether we could trace the noises back to a human.

For nights and nights, we sat up till two or three o'clock in the morning. No logical explanation for the noises could be found.

I decided to test a theory I had. On Christmas Eve, the anniversary of Mr. Jeremy Lester's disappearance, I would stay up and keep watch by myself in the red bedroom.

In the darkness of the night, I sat in the red room. For over an hour, I might as well have been in my grave, for that's as much as I could see of the haunted chamber.

As the minutes passed, I sat on, but still, no sound broke the silence. I was weary with many nights' watching and tired of my solitary vigil. I slipped into a light slumber from which I was awakened by hearing the door softly open.

"John?" my sister whispered. "John, are you here?"

"Yes, Clare," I answered. "What are you doing up at this hour?"

"Come downstairs," she replied. "They are in the oak parlor."

I did not need any explanation as to whom she meant. We crept downstairs together—no mouse could have pursued its way along the corridor with greater silence and caution than the pair of us.

By the open door of the oak room, Clare paused, and we both looked in.

The room we had left in the darkness was illuminated with a bright wood fire blazing on the hearth. We could see candles along the mantle, and the small table was pulled away from its usual corner, and two men sat at it, playing cribbage.

We could see the face of the younger player—he was about twenty-five years old with the mischievous face of a man who liked to live wickedly. He was dressed in the costume of a bygone period—his hair was powdered, and around his wrists were ruffles of lace. On his little finger, there sparkled a ring. On the front of his shirt, a diamond gleamed, and on each of his shoes, diamond buckles. It was at that moment, in the amber glow of the fire, that I stared upon the face of my ancestor, Jeremy Lester. It would be difficult for me to say how I knew this, how in a moment, I identified the features of the player with those of a man who had been missing for forty-one years... forty-one years that very night.

As we continued to watch, I couldn't help but think that Jeremy Lester looked like someone who had just returned from some great party and decided to return home and play a game of cards with a dear friend.

He sat opposite the door but never once lifted his eyes to it. His attention was focused on the cards.

For a time, there was complete silence in the oak room, broken only by the monotonous counting of the game.

In the doorway, we stood, holding our breath, terrified, yet fascinated by the scene playing out before us.

The ashes fell from the hearth softly like snow. We could hear the rustle of the cards as they were dealt out and fell upon the table. We listened to the count: fifteen-one, fifteen-two, and so on. No other words were spoken until the player whose face we could not see exclaimed, "I win! The game is mine!"

Jeremy Lester took up the cards, looking them over before flinging the whole pack into his guest's face. "Cheater! Liar!"

There was a struggle. Chairs were flung out of the way, cards flew through the air, and the two men fought, their passionate voices mingling so that we could not hear a sentence of what they were shouting.

All of a sudden, Jeremy Lester marched from the room in such a hurry, he almost touched us where we stood. He left the room, stomped up the staircase, and disappeared into the red room before returning with a pair of rapiers under his arm.

When he reentered the room, he gave the other man his choice of weapons before flinging the window open and walking forth into the cold night air. Clare and I followed.

We went through the garden and down a narrow winding path to a smooth piece of grass sheltered from the chill by a grove of trees. By this time, the moon was shining bright, and we could distinctly see Jeremy Lester measuring along the ground.

"When you say 'three,'" he said to the man whose back was still toward us.

"One," began the cheating companion. "Two," but before our kinsman had the slightest suspicion of his friend's plan, his rapier pierced through Jeremy Lester's breast.

At the sight of the cowardly treachery, Clare screamed. At that moment, the phantoms vanished, the moon was obscured behind a cloud, and we were standing in the shadow of the trees, shivering with cold and terror.

But we knew at last what had become of the late owner of Martingdale—that he had fallen, not in a fair fight, but foully murdered by a false friend.

When I awoke late on Christmas morning, it was to see a white world, behold the ground, trees, and shrubs all laden and covered with snow. There was snow everywhere, such snow as no person could remember having fallen in forty-one years.

"It was on just such a Christmas as this that Mr. Jeremy disappeared," I overheard the caretaker whisper to his wife.

For the New Year, Clare and I were dining at Cronson Park, when all of a sudden, my sister dropped the glass of water she was carrying to her lips and exclaimed, "Look, John! There he is!" while pointing to a portrait hanging on the wall. "I saw him for an instant when he turned his head toward the door as Jeremy Lester left it. That's him, I'm sure of it."

Of what followed after this revelation, I have only the vaguest recollection. Servants scurried about. Mrs. Cronson dropped to her chair in a fit of hysterics. The daughters gathered around their mother. Clare begged to be taken away. Mr. Cronson bumbled through some kind of explanation.

He told me that the portrait Clare identified was of his wife's father, Mr. Wharley, the last person to see Jeremy Lester alive.

"He is an old man now," Mr. Cronson finished. "A man of over eighty, who has confessed everything to me. I trust you won't bring further disgrace upon the Cronson family by making this matter public?"

I promised, but the story gradually oozed out, and the Cronsons left the country.

Years have now passed, and I am still the resident master of Martingdale. The young lady Clare wanted me to "think seriously of" is now my wife and the mother of my children.

Sadly, my sister never returned Martingdale, even though I assure her there are no strange noises in the house anymore. No footsteps on the stairs, no furniture banging about, and no phantoms in the night… not even on Christmas Eve.

Mock Turtle Soup

Inspired by an 1845 Recipe

Ingredients:
1 lb of stew meat
1 large onion, minced
4 tbsp of butter
1 garlic clove, minced
3 cloves
¼ tsp of thyme
1 bay leaf
¼ tsp of rosemary
1 tsp of black peppercorns
¼ tsp of ground mace
¼ tsp of cayenne pepper
¼ cup of flour
6 cups of beef broth
Salt and pepper to taste
½ cup of sherry
½ cup of heavy cream
½ of a lemon, cut into slices with rind

Directions:
1. Brown the meat.
2. Sauté the onions in butter. Add garlic, cloves, thyme, rosemary, the bay leaf, peppercorns, mace, and cayenne.
3. Stir in flour and make a roux.
4. Gradually add the hot broth.

5. Salt and pepper to taste. Add lemon and meat. Bring to a boil.
6. Simmer for two hours, stirring occasionally.
7. Add cream and sherry. Simmer for another 30 minutes.

Mock turtle soup is an English and American soup that acted as a substitute for green turtle soup.

Dating back to the 1720s, green turtle soup became popular when sailors brought the turtles back from the West Indies. The soup was an instant hit, and the upper class (particularly the royal family) became so obsessed with this exotic and expensive new dish that the turtles were nearly hunted to extinction.

Less wealthy families in England and America opted for mock turtle soup that eventually became more popular than the original green turtle soup (Heinz and Campbell's even made commercialized versions in a can).

Mock turtle soup was served at Abraham Lincoln's first inauguration. It was considered the ultimate comfort food, appearing on most tables not just at Christmas time but throughout the years until its popularity died out in the 1960s.

The original recipe of mock turtle soup calls for calf's head and other organs, but we figured stew meat is easier to come by at your local grocery store.

The Mistletoe Bough
By: Thomas Haynes Bayly
C.1830

The mistletoe hung in the castle hall,
The holly branch shone on the old oak wall;
And the baron's retainers were blithe and gay,
And keeping their Christmas holiday.
The baron beheld, with a father's pride,
His beautiful child, young Lovell's bride;
While she, with her bright eye, seemed to be
The star of goodly company.

"I'm weary of dancing now," she cried:
"Here tarry a moment—I'll hide—I'll hide!
And, Lovell, be sure thou'rt first to trace
The clue to my secret lurking-place."
Away she ran—and her friends began
Each tower to search, and each nook to scan;
And young Lovell cried, "Oh! Where dost thou hide?
I'm lonely without thee, my own dear bride."

They sought her that night, and they sought her next day;

And they sought her in vain, when a week passed away!

In the highest—the lowest—the loneliest spot,

Young Lovell sought wildly—but found her not.

And years flew by, and their grief at last

Was told as a sorrowful tale long past;

And when Lovell appeared, the children cried,

"See! The old man weeps for his fairy bride."

At length an oak chest, that had long lain hid,

Was found in the castle; they raised the lid;

And a skeleton form lay moldering there

In the bridal wreath of that lady fair!

Oh, sad was her fate! In sportive jest

She hid from her lord in the old oak chest;

It closed with a spring!—and, dreadful doom,

The bride lay clasped in her living tomb!

The Old Nurse's Story
By: Elizabeth Gaskell
1852

You know, my dears, that your mother was an orphan and an only child. I'm sure you've heard that your grandfather was a clergyman up in Westmorland, where I come from. I was just a girl in the village school when one day, your grandmother came in to ask the mistress if there were any students there who would make a good nurse-maid. I was so proud when the mistress called me up and spoke about my being good at my needlework and a steady, honest girl whose family was respectable, even though they were poor. I thought to myself that I would want nothing more than to serve this beautiful young woman, who was blushing as deep as I was as she spoke of the coming baby and what I should have to do with it.

I can see you don't care much for this part of the story. Well, I was hired and settled at the parsonage before Miss Rosamond (that was the baby who is now your mother) was born. To be honest, I had very little to do with her when she first arrived, for she never left her mother's arms and slept with her all night long. But I was so proud when the missis would trust me with her.

There was never such a fine and happy baby before or since. You were all fine enough in your own ways, but for sweet, winning ways, none of you come close to your mother. She took after her mother, who was a real lady.

When your mother, little Miss Rosamond, was about four or five years old, both of her parents died within a fortnight of each other. What a sad time that was. The mistress and I were both looking forward to the birth of her second baby when my master came home from one of his long rides, wet and tired and came down with the fever that killed him… and then she never held her head up again. She lived long enough to see her dead baby laid on her breast before she breathed her last breath. On her deathbed, she asked me to never leave Miss Rosamond. But even if she hadn't asked this of me, I would have followed the little girl to the ends of the earth.

The next morning, long before we had stopped crying, the executors and guardians came to settle the estate. In attendance was my poor young mistress's own cousin, Lord

Furnivall, and Mr. Esthwaite, my master's brother and shopkeeper in Manchester. I don't know if it was part of their will or if my mistress had written to her cousin on her deathbed, but it was decided that Miss Rosamond and I were to go to Furnivall Manor in Northumberland. Lord Furnivall said that it had been Miss Rosamond's mother's dying wish that she would live with his family, and what was one more person in so grand a household? I was too hasty in sharing the news in town that I was to be a young lady's maid at Lord Furnivall's manor.

I was mistaken to think that we were going to live where my lord did. It turned out that the family had left Furnivall Manor fifty years prior. The manor house was at the foot of the Cumberland Fells and a very grand place. Apparently, an old Miss Furnivall (a great-aunt of my lord's) lived there with a few servants. My lord thought that the old place might suit Miss Rosamond for a few years and that her being there might amuse his old aunt.

My lord told me to have Miss Rosamond's things ready by a certain day. He was a stern, proud man (as all the Lord Furnivalls were), and he never spoke a word more than was necessary. Folks did say that he had loved my young mistress, but because she knew his father would object, she married Mr. Esthwaite instead. He never married, but he took an instant shining to Miss Rosamond, which made me think there was some truth to the rumors… perhaps he truly did love her mother.

He sent his gentleman with us to the manor house but ordered him to join him at Newcastle later that night, so there was not much time for the gentleman to introduce us to all the strangers before he, too, left us. We were two lonely young things (I was not even eighteen yet) in the great old manor house.

It seems like just yesterday we drove there. We had left our beloved parsonage early in the morning, crying. It was past noon on a September day when we drove up the lane to the manor house. We had left all signs of a town, or even a village, and were then inside the gates of a large wild park not like the parks here in the north. This park was filled with rocks, and the sound of running water, and gnarled thorned trees, and old oaks all white and peeled with age.

The road went up about two miles, and then we saw a great and stately house, with trees close around it—so close that in some places, their branches dragged against the walls when the wind blew. No one seemed to take care of the place to chop wood or keep the moss-covered carriage house in order. Only the front of the house was all clear. The great drive was without a single weed, and neither tree nor vine was allowed to grow over the many-windowed façade. Although the house was desolate, it was even grander than I expected. Behind it rose the Fells, and to the left of the house was a little old-fashioned flower garden.

As we entered the front hall, I feared that we may become lost in the house—it was so large and vast and grand. There was a chandelier of bronze hanging down from the middle of the ceiling. I had never seen one before and looked at it, amazed. At one end of the hall was a great fireplace as large as some houses in my hometown, and by it were large old-fashioned sofas. At the opposite end of the hall was an organ built into the wall, so large that it filled up the best part of that end. Beyond it, on the same side, was a door.

The afternoon was closing in, and the hall, which had no fire to illuminate it, was dark and gloomy, but we didn't stay there for even a moment. The servant who had opened the door for us took us through the door beside the organ and led us through several smaller halls into the west drawing-room. It was there that Miss Furnivall was to meet us.

Poor little Miss Rosamond clung to me as if she were scared and lost in such a great place. As for myself, I felt the same.

The west drawing-room was very cheerful, with a warm fire in the hearth and plenty of comfortable furniture. Miss Furnivall was almost eighty years old. She was thin and tall and had a face full of wrinkles. Her eyes were piercing as she watched us (no doubt to make up for her being so deaf she needed to use a trumpet). Sitting with her, working on a great piece of tapestry, was Mrs. Stark, her maid and companion, almost as old as she was. She had lived with Miss Furnivall ever since they were both young, and now she seemed more like a friend than a servant. She looked so cold and gray and stony as if she had never loved or cared for anyone other than her mistress (and with Miss Furnivall's deafness, Mrs. Stark treated her very much like a child). Our gentleman gave some message from my lord and then bowed goodbye. He left without even noticing my sweet little Miss Rosamond's outstretched hand.

I was relieved when the two old ladies rung for the footman to take us up to our rooms. So, we left the great drawing-room and into another sitting room, out of that and then up a flight of stairs, and along a gallery which looked more like a library with shelves of books, until we came to our room. I began to think I would be lost in this house for days.

There was an old nursery that had been used for all the little lords and ladies long ago, with a pleasant fire burning in the grate, and the kettle was already boiling with things for tea spread out on the table. Connected to that room was a bedroom with a little crib for Miss Rosamond close to my bed.

Old James (the servant) called up his wife, Dorothy, to welcome us. They were both so hospitable and kind that Miss Rosamond and I gradually began to feel at home. By the time tea was over, she was sitting on Dorothy's lap and chattering away as fast as her little tongue could muster.

I soon found out that Dorothy was from Westmorland—binding us together. James had lived almost his entire life in my lord's family. Together, they had one servant working under them—Bessy.

We quickly became a little family—Bessy, myself, Miss Rosamond, James, Dorothy, Miss Furnivall, and Mrs. Stark. The hard, sad Miss Furnivall and the cold Mrs. Stark always lit up whenever Rosamond came fluttering into a room. I am sure they were sorry to see her go whenever she would dash off to the kitchen, but they were just too proud to ask her to stay with them. Miss Rosamond made the house her kingdom—setting out on expeditions all over it, with me at her heels (all except the east wing, which was never opened, nor did we have any desire to go there). But there was plenty for us to see in the northern and western part of the house, each room filled with curiosities. The windows were darkened by the sweeping boughs of the trees and the ivy which had overgrown them, but in the green gloom, we managed to see old China jars, canned ivory boxes, great heavy books, and above all else, old pictures.

I remember my darling would run to Dorothy and have her tell us who they all were, for they were portraits of my lord's family. She would try but couldn't tell us the names of everyone. We had explored all of the rooms when we came to the old state drawing-room over the hall, and there was a picture of Miss Furnivall, or as she was called back in those days, Miss Grace, for she was the younger sister. What a beauty she was! Though hidden behind the beauty was such scorn and pride.

"Gracious!" I said as I stared up at the young Miss Furnivall's face. "Who would have thought that Miss Furnivall had been such a beauty back in her day!"

"Yes," Dorothy said. "Folks change. But if what my master's father says is true, Miss Furnival—the elder sister—was even more beautiful than Miss Grace. Her picture is here somewhere. If I show it to you, you must never tell anyone—not even James. Can the little lady hold her tongue?"

I was not sure, for Miss Rosamond was such a bold and outspoken child, so I told her to hide somewhere and then helped Dorothy turn around a great picture that faced the wall. Strange that it was not hung up with the others.

To be sure, it beat Miss Grace for beauty and for the scornful pride too. I could have looked at it for much longer, but Miss Dorothy seemed frightened. She quickly spun it back toward the wall and told me to run and look for Miss Rosamond. She warned that there were some dangerous and ugly places in the house that no child should venture. I was a brave, high-spirited girl and thought little of what the old woman said—for I too liked hide-and-seek. I ran off to find my little one.

As winter drew on, the days grew shorter. There were moments when I was almost certain I heard a noise as if someone was playing on the great organ in the hall. I did not hear it every evening, but often enough… usually when I was sitting with Miss Rosamond after I had put her to bed.

The first night when I went down to my supper, I asked Dorothy who had been playing music. James was very quick to say that it was just the trees scratching at the windows, but I saw Dorothy look at him quite fearfully. Even Bessy, the kitchen-maid, said something under her breath. I saw that they did not like my question, so I didn't say any more on the subject until I knew I could talk to Dorothy in private.

The next day, I tried to ask her again about who was playing the organ the night before—for I knew that it was the organ and not the wind. But Dorothy was well-trained by her husband and didn't say a word. So I tried Bessy, who was quick to buckle under pressure.

She made me promise never to tell and that if I ever did tell anyone, I was never to say that I heard it from her. She said that it was a very strange noise, and she heard it many times herself—mostly on wintery nights before a storm. Folks said that it was the old lord playing on the organ in the great hall, just as he used to do when he was alive. But who the "old lord" was or why he played (particularly on stormy winter nights), she either could not or would not tell me.

Well, I told you I was a brave girl. I thought it was rather pleasant to have the grand music echo through the house, no matter who the player was. It rose above the gusts of wind, growing loud and soft with its melodies and tunes... What nonsense to say it was the wind!

I thought perhaps it was Miss Furnivall who played, unknown to Bessy. But one day, when I was in the hall by myself, I opened the organ and looked all around it. I was shocked to find it broken and destroyed inside. Even though it was the middle of the afternoon, my skin began to crawl. I quickly shut it back up and ran away to the bright nursery. From that moment on, just like James and Dorothy, I did not like hearing the music.

All this time, Miss Rosamond was making herself more and more beloved. The old ladies liked having her dine with them at dinner, and afterward, she would play in the corner of the great drawing-room while Miss Furnival dozed. She was a good girl but always liked returning to me in the nursery afterward. She said that Miss Furnivall was so sad and Mrs. Stark was so dull. Together, she and I would play and be merry. Eventually, I ignored the distant organ music, for it did no one any harm as long as you didn't stop to think about where it was coming from.

That winter was very cold. In the middle of October, the frosts began and lasted for weeks. One day at dinner, Miss Furnivall lifted her sad, heavy eyes and said to Mrs. Stark, "I am afraid we shall have a terrible winter," in a strange way. But Mrs. Stark pretended not to hear and talked loudly of something else.

My little lady and I did not care much for the frost. As long as it was dry outside, we played and raced and ran outside behind the house. The air was sharp and fresh. But the days grew shorter, and the old lord (if it *was* he) played more frequently on the organ.

One Sunday afternoon near the end of November, I asked Dorothy to watch Miss Rosamond so I could go to church—it was much too cold for the child to go. Bessy and I set off very briskly under the heavy black sky.

"We shall have a fall of snow," Bessy said to me.

Sure enough, even while we were in church, it came down thick, in great large flakes, so thick it almost darkened the windows.

It had stopped snowing by the time we came out, but it lay soft and thick beneath our feet as we marched home.

Before we got to the hall, the moon rose—I think it was brighter with the moonlight reflecting off the snow than when we first set out to church around two o'clock.

I forgot to tell you that Miss Furnivall and Mrs. Stark never went to church. Sometimes they would read the prayers together, but they would spend most of their day in the drawing-room, taking a break from their tapestry work. So when I went to Dorothy in the kitchen to fetch Miss Rosamond, I did not worry when she told me that the ladies had kept the child with them in the drawing-room.

I took off my things and went to find her and bring her her supper in the nursery. But when I went into the drawing-room, there sat two old ladies, very quiet and still. I thought the child might be hiding from me—it was a game she liked to play—and she had somehow managed to convince the old ladies to look as if they knew nothing about her. I went softly throughout the room, peeking under the sofa and behind a chair, pretending that I was sad and frightened while looking for her.

"What's the matter, Hester?" Mrs. Stark asked sharply.

I wasn't sure if Miss Furnivall had seen me. As I told you, she was very deaf, and she sat quite still, staring into the fire with a hopeless face.

"I'm just looking for my little Rosy-Posy," I replied, still thinking that the child was there, near me, though I couldn't see her.

"Miss Rosamond is not here," Mrs. Stark said. "She went to find Dorothy over an hour ago."

My heart sank at this, and I suddenly wished I had never left the child to go to church. I ran back to Dorothy and told her. James was out for the day, but she, me, and Bessy took lights and went up to the nursery before roaming over the great house, calling for Miss Rosamond to come out of her hiding place. But there was no answer... no sound.

"Could she have gone to the east wing?" I asked at last. "Could she be hiding there?"

But Dorothy said that was impossible. She, herself, had never been there, and the doors were always locked, and only the lord's steward had the keys.

I said I would go back to the drawing-room and see if she was perhaps hiding in there, unbeknownst to the old ladies.

As I entered the west drawing-room, I told Mrs. Stark that we could not find her anywhere. I asked for permission to search the room and was frightened not to find her anywhere. Even Miss Furnivall got up and looked, trembling all over. We set off once again—everyone in the house—looking in all the places we had searched before, but we could not find her.

Miss Furnivall shivered and shook so much that Mrs. Stark took her back into the warm drawing-room, but not before they made me promise to bring Rosamond to them when she was found. I feared she may never be found.

While I was upstairs, I glanced out the window down into the great frontcourt. It was dark outside, but the snow was illuminated in the moonlight. I could see two little footprints running from the hall door and around the corner of the east wing.

I don't know how I got downstairs so fast, but I tugged open the great, stiff hall door, and throwing the skirt of my gown over my head for a cloak, I ran outside.

Turning the east corner, I saw a black shadow falling across the snow. As I ran further, I noticed the footprints going up to the Fells. It was bitter cold—so cold that the air almost took the skin off my face as I ran—but I ran on, fearing that my little mistress must be so frightened... or worse.

At that moment, I saw a shepherd coming down the hill toward me, carrying something wrapped up in his arms. He shouted to me, asking if I had lost a *bairn*. I collapsed to the ground, crying, and he ran to me.

I looked up and saw my wee *bairn* lying still and white and stiff in his arms as if she was dead.

He told me he had been up in the Fells gathering his sheep before the deep freeze of the night came when he spotted my little darling stiff and cold, huddled under a pair of holly trees.

Oh, the joy and tears of having her in my arms again! I would not let him carry her. I took her, still wrapped in his blanket, and quickly made my way to the kitchen door.

"Bring the warming-pan!" I ordered as I carried her upstairs and began undressing her by the nursery fire. I called her all the sweet and playful names I could think of even while my eyes were blinded by tears. At last, she opened her large blue eyes. I put her into her warm bed and then sent Dorothy down to tell Miss Furnivall that all was well and that I had made up my mind to sit by my darling's bedside for the rest of the night. She drifted into a soft sleep as soon as her head touched the pillow, and I watched her until morning. As the sun rose, I couldn't help but think that she awoke bright and clear... at least that's what I thought at first.

She explained that the night before, she wanted to see Dorothy since both the old ladies were resting and it was very dull in the drawing-room. As she was going through the west lobby, she saw the snow falling soft and steady through the window, but she wanted to see it lying pretty and white on the ground. So, she made her way into the great hall and stared out the window. While she stared at the snow, bright and soft upon the drive, she saw a little girl.

"She waved to me," my little darling said. "She wanted me to come outside with her." She told me that this other little girl had taken her by the hand, and the two of them made their way around the east corner of the house.

"Why would you make up such a story?" I shook my head at her. "I know your mamma never taught you to lie like this."

"I'm telling you the truth!" the child sobbed. "You have to believe me!"

"Believe you?" I scoffed, my voice stern. "I followed your footprints through the snow, and there was only one set—yours. If you had been walking hand-in-hand with another little girl, don't you think there would have been another pair of footprints next to yours?"

"Please, Hester!" she cried. "I never looked at her feet, but she held my hand so tight. Her skin was so very cold. She took me up the path to the Fells, up to the holly trees. There was a lady crying, but when she saw us, she stopped and smiled at me. She picked me up and lulled me to sleep... that's all. Please, Hester," she begged me. "It's true! My mamma knows I'm telling the truth."

I thought perhaps she was in a fever, so I pretended to believe her. She told the story over and over again, and it was always the same.

At last, Dorothy knocked on the door with Miss Rosamond's breakfast. She told me that the old ladies were down eating their breakfast, and they both wished to speak to me.

This is it, I thought to myself as I made my way to the north gallery. I feared they would blame me for losing Rosamond. *But she was in their care when I left, and it was their fault they let her sneak away.*

I went into the room boldly and told my story. I stood before Miss Furnivall, shouting Rosamond's tale close to her ear. When I came to the part where the other little girl appeared in the snow, coaxing Rosamond outside to the beautiful lady near the holly tree, the old woman threw up her old, withered arms and cried out, "Oh! Heaven! Have mercy!"

Mrs. Stark grabbed her, but she was beyond Mrs. Stark's control as she spoke to me with a wild warning:

"Hester! Keep her away from that child! That evil child will lure her to her death! Tell Rosamond that she is a naughty, wicked child."

Mrs. Stark pushed me from the room, and I was glad to go—my heart pounding in my chest. I could still hear Miss

Furnivall shrieking, "Oh! Have mercy! Will you never forgive even after all these years?"

From that moment on, I was uneasy in the house. I never left Miss Rosamond's side, day or night, for fear she might slip off again. I wasn't sure if I feared the phantom child Rosamond thought she saw or Miss Furnivall's madness. In my heart, I even feared that some sort of madness haunted the family... even my little Rosamond.

The great frost never ended, and the storms continued to roll in... always accompanied by the old lord playing on the great organ. But old lord or not, wherever Miss Rosamond went, I followed—my love for her was stronger than my fear for the grand terrible sound. We played together and wandered together, here, there, and everywhere. I never dared to lose sight of her in that large, rambling house.

Not long before Christmas Day, we were playing together at the billiard table in the great hall. By and by, without our noticing, the afternoon turned into dusk, and I thought of taking her back to the nursery when, all of a sudden, she cried out:

"Look, Hester! There is that poor little girl out in the snow!"

I turned toward the windows and, sure enough, I saw a little girl without a coat or shawl crying in the bitter cold, beating her hands against the window panes as if she wanted to be let in. There was something wrong with the child outside the window—in the stillness of the dead-cold weather, I couldn't hear the battering of her hands on the glass, nor the sound of her crying. She sobbed and wailed until Miss Rosamond could bear it no longer.

She ran to open the door when the great organ suddenly pealed out so loud and thundered all around us—the sound cut through to my heart. I trembled and was frozen in horror.

A crescendo in the organ music brought me back to life. I ran after Miss Rosamond and caught her before she could open the hall door. I clutched her tight and carried her away, kicking and screaming, into the large bright kitchen, where Dorothy and Bessy were busy with their mince pies.

"What's the matter with the little one?" Dorothy cried out as I carried Miss Rosamond into the room, who was still sobbing as if her heart was breaking.

"She won't let me open the door for the little girl! She'll die if she stays out on the Fells all night!" Rosamond sobbed, slapping me. I glanced at Dorothy to see a look of ghastly terror on her face… it made my very blood run cold.

"Shut the back kitchen door fast and bolt it," she ordered Bessy. Saying no more, she offered raisins and almonds to quiet Miss Rosamond.

I was relieved when Miss Rosamond cried herself to sleep. After I tucked the child into her bed, I snuck back down to the kitchen and told Dorothy that I had made up my mind. I would bring Rosamond back to my father's house in Applethwaite, where we could live in peace. I told her I had been frightened enough by the blasted organ playing. But now that I had seen this moaning child for myself, silently beating against the window to get in, I couldn't stay there any longer.

The color drained from Dorothy's face. When I had finished speaking, she told me that she didn't think I could take Miss Rosamond with me—she was my lord's ward, and I had no right over her.

"Will you leave the child you clearly love so much," she asked me, "all because you've seen and heard some things that can't hurt you? We've all had to accept it."

"Why do I have the feeling that you had to accept these things because you all had something to do with this specter child while she was alive?"

I instantly regretted my words as Dorothy told me all that she knew. Her words were unbelievable, and yet I became more afraid than ever.

She said that she heard the tale from the old neighbors that were alive when she first married James and came to live at the manor. Back then, people still came to the hall, before it got such a bad name in the countryside.

"It might be true," she shrugged her shoulders as she began her tale. "Or it might not."

The "old lord" was Miss Furnivall's father—Miss Grace, as Dorothy called her, for, in this story, Miss Maude was the elder sister and Miss Furnivall by all rights.

The old lord was a proud man—prouder than any man you've ever seen or heard of—and his daughters were just like him. No one was good enough to marry them, although they had plenty of suitors—for they were the most beautiful ladies of their day.

But as the old saying goes, "Pride will have a fall," and these two beauties fell in love with the same man. He was a simple foreign musician their father had hired from London to play at the manor house. For, above all things, next to his pride, the old lord loved music. He could play on almost every instrument, yet the music never seemed to soften him. He was a fierce old man who had broken his wife's heart with his cruelty. He was mad for music and would pay any amount of money for it.

So, he hired the young musician to come. He made such beautiful music, they say the very birds in the trees stopped singing just to listen. He was such a talented young man, the foreign musician was ordered to come every year to play for the family. He had the great organ sent over from Holland and built in the hall where it still stands. He taught the old lord to play on it. While Lord Furnivall was busy playing music on his organ, the musician was walking in the woods with one of the young ladies—first Miss Maude and then Miss Grace.

Miss Maude won the day. She and the handsome young musician were married, unknown to anyone. Before he returned for his yearly visit, she was secretly living in a farmhouse on the moors with a little girl while her father and Miss Grace thought she was away at Doncaster Races.

Even though she was a wife and mother, she was not a bit softened but as hot and passionate as ever. Perhaps even more so. She was jealous of Miss Grace, whom her husband still paid a great deal of attention to.

It seemed Miss Grace triumphed over Miss Maude and Miss Maude grew fiercer and fiercer, both with her husband and her sister. The musician had a habit of running away when Miss Maude grew passionate, hiding himself in foreign countries. After one particularly passionate argument, he decided to leave a month earlier than usual and threatened never to return.

Meanwhile, the little girl was left in the farmhouse while her mother still lived in the manor. Once a week, Miss Maude would have her horse saddled and gallop wildly over the hills to see her. Where she loved, she loved, and where she hated, she hated. She hated the girl and hated the child's father.

And the old lord went on playing on his organ. The servants thought his sweet music had finally soothed his awful temper. He grew weak and infirm and had to walk with a crutch. His son (the present Lord Furnivall's father) was with the army in America, and his other son was at sea, so Miss Maude was alone. She and Miss Grace grew colder and more bitter toward each other every day till, at last, they hardly ever spoke.

The foreign musician returned again the following summer, but it was for the last time. The sisters' jealousy and bickering drove him away, and he was never heard from again. Miss Maude, who had always meant to acknowledge her marriage only after her father was dead, was now left a deserted wife with a child that no one knew about. Living with a father she feared and a sister she hated, she didn't dare admit to the child's existence.

When the next summer came and went, and the handsome foreigner never came, both Miss Maude and Miss Grace grew gloomy and sad—they both had a haggard look about them though they were both still as beautiful as ever.

Over time, Miss Maude managed to forget her husband. Her father grew older and weaker and more than ever obsessed with his music. She and Miss Grace lived almost entirely apart, having separate rooms. Miss Grace was in the west rooms and Miss Maude in the east rooms (the very rooms which are now shut up). At this point, Miss Maude thought that she might have her little girl live with her, and no one ever needed to know. If anyone asked, the girl was a local child Miss Maude had taken a fancy to.

"Everyone around here knows this part of the story," Dorothy explained. "It's what came afterward that no one knows for sure. No one except Miss Grace and Mrs. Stark, who was her maid even then."

According to the servants, Miss Maude mocked Miss Grace, telling her that the entire time the musician was pretending to love her, he was already married to herself. The color left Miss Grace's face and never returned. She was heard saying many times that sooner or later, she would take her revenge, and Mrs. Stark was forever spying in the east rooms.

One fearful night, just after the New Year had come in, when the snow was lying thick and deep, and the flakes were still falling—fast enough to blind anyone who might be outside—there was a violent noise that shook the house. The old lord's voice echoed above it all, cursing, along with the cries of a small child and the proud shouts of a fierce woman. There was a scuffle, a blow, and a dead stillness as the moans and wails died away on the hillside.

The old lord summoned all his servants and told them that his daughter had disgraced herself and that he had thrown her out—her and her child—and that if any of them ever offered her help or food or shelter, that would be the end of them. All the while, Miss Grace stood beside him, white and still as a statue. When he was finished, she heaved a great sigh as if to say that her work was done.

The old lord never touched his organ again, and he died within the year. It's no wonder, though—the day after that wild and fearful night, the shepherds found Miss Maude sitting, crazed and smiling, under the holly trees, nursing a dead child.

"It was the frost and the cold that killed the child." Dorothy shook her head. "Now you know the truth... Are you less frightened now?"

I was more frightened than ever, but I said I was not. I wished Miss Rosamond and I could leave that dreadful house forever, but I would not leave her, and I didn't dare to take her away. But oh! How I watched her and guarded her!

We bolted the doors and shuttered the windows an hour before dark rather than leave them open five minutes too late. But my little lady still heard the phantom child crying, and I could say nothing to keep her from wanting to go to the girl and let her in from the cruel wind and snow.

All this time, I kept away from Miss Furnivall and Mrs. Stark. I knew no good could come from either of them with their dark hard faces and their dreamy eyes looking back at the ghastly years that were long gone. But even in my fear, I pitied Miss Furnivall as you pity one who has committed a deadly sin, and you know their soul is doomed.

One night—just after New Years' Day had come at last, and the long winter had taken a turn—I heard the west drawing-room bell ring three times, which was a signal for me. I would not leave Miss Rosamond alone (for the old lord was playing wilder than ever, and I feared the specter child would take my darling), so I took her from her bed and wrapped her in a blanket before carrying her down to the drawing-room where the old ladies sat at their tapestry work as usual.

They looked up when I came in, and Mrs. Stark asked, surprised, "Why did you bring Miss Rosamond here out of her warm bed?"

I began to whisper, "I was afraid she would be tempted outside while I was away by the child in the snow—"

Mrs. Stark stopped me with a glance at Miss Furnivall before telling me Miss Furnivall wanted me to undo some work she had done wrong (which neither of them could see to unpick).

I laid the child on the sofa and sat down on a stool by them, hardening my heart against them as I heard the wind howling.

Miss Furnivall never said a word nor looked around when the gusts shook the windows. All of a sudden, she stood up to her full height.

"I hear voices!" she said, her voice shaking. "Terrible screams! Father's voice!"

At that moment, Rosamond woke with a start. "My little girl is crying!" She tried to get up and go to her, but her feet tangled in the blanket, and I managed to catch her.

My flesh began to crawl at these noises, which they both heard so clearly, but I couldn't hear a sound.

It took a minute, but the noises came, gathered fast, and filled our ears. At last, we all heard the voices and screams, no longer the winter's wind that raged outside.

Mrs. Stark looked at me and I at her, but we didn't dare to speak.

Suddenly Miss Furnivall went to the door, out of the room, through the west lobby, and opened the door into the great hall. Mrs. Stark followed, and I (desperate to not be left behind) followed as well though my heart nearly stopped beating in fear. I wrapped my darling tight in my arms and went after them.

In the hall, the screams were louder than ever. It seemed as if they came from the east wing, coming closer on the other side of the locked door.

Then I noticed that the great bronze chandelier seemed to be illuminated, though the hall was dim, and that a fire was blazing in the hearth, though it gave off no heat. I shuddered with terror and held Rosamond closer to my chest. But as I did so, the east door shook, and she suddenly struggled to get away from me. "Hester, I must go!" she screamed. "My little girl is here—I hear her! She's coming!"

I held her tight with all my strength. I'm sure that if I had died, my hands would have grasped her still, I was so determined to keep her safe.

Miss Furnivall stood listening and didn't pay any attention to the child, who had managed to slip out of my arms. I knelt on my knees, holding tightly to her still, even as she fought to break free.

All at once, the east door gave way with a thunderous crash, as if torn open in a rage, and the figure of a tall old man stood in the mysterious light. He had gray hair and gleaming eyes. Behind him, he dragged a beautiful woman and a little child clinging to her dress.

"Oh, Hester!" Miss Rosamond cried. "It's the lady! The lady from the holly trees, and my little girl is with her! Hester, let me go to her. I must go!"

She convulsed as she tried to get away, but I held her tighter and tighter until I feared I might hurt her. I preferred that to letting her go toward those terrible phantoms.

They passed us, marching toward the great hall door where the winds howled. But, before they reached the door, the lady turned, and I could see that she defied the old man with a proud and fierce spirit. She threw herself in front of her child to protect her from a blow from the old man.

And Rosamond continued to pull away from me as if by some sort of unseen power.

"They want me to go with them to the Fells. They are drawing me to them. Little girl!" she called out, her voice growing faint. "I would come with you, but Hester won't let go!"

When she saw the old man raise his crutch to strike the mother and child, she fainted away, and I thanked God for it.

Just at this moment, when the tall old man, his hair hanging low across his sweaty brow, was going to strike the shrinking child, Miss Furnivall (the old woman standing at my side) cried out, "Oh father! Spare the innocent child!"

It was then I saw—we all saw—another phantom appear and grow out of the blue and misty light that filled the hall. We had not seen her until now, for it was another lady who stood by the old man with a look of such hate and triumphant scorn. That figure was so beautiful, with a soft white hat drawn down over the proud brows and red curling lip. It was dressed in a robe of blue satin. I had seen the figure before... it looked just like Miss Furnivall in her youth.

The terrible phantoms continued on, regardless of Miss Furnivall's wild and desperate pleas, and the uplifted crutch struck the child. The young sister looked on, silent and serene.

At that moment, the dim lights and the fire that gave no heat went out, and Miss Furnivall lay at our feet, struck down by the horrifying scene.

Yes! She was carried away to her bed that night and never woke up again. She lay with her face to the wall, muttering, "What is done in youth can never be undone in age! What is done in youth can never be undone in age!"

Mince Pies
Inspired by a Recipe from 1827

Ingredients for Mincemeat:
8 oz of chopped raisins
8 oz of currants
8 oz of granulated sugar
8 oz of grated beef suet (or vegetable shortening)
8 oz of peeled and grated apple
4 oz of sultanas
2 oz of candied peel
½ wine glass of brandy
½ wine glass of sherry
1 tsp of mace
1 tsp of nutmeg
1 tsp of cinnamon
Juice and rind of one lemon

Directions:
1827 style:
1. Add all the ingredients to a mixing bowl, cover, and leave to stand overnight.
2. The following morning mix thoroughly and place in jars.
3. Leave of 1-2 months before using.

2021 style:
1. Cook raisins, currants, suet (or shortening), apples, sultanas, and peel with sugar slowly for 90 minutes.
2. Add spices and alcohol.

Ingredients for Pastry:
1 cup of flour
1 stick of cold butter, cubed
3 tbsp of ice water
½ tsp of salt
4-6 tsp of milk
1 tsp of sugar

Directions:
1. Sift the flour and salt into a large mixing bowl.
2. Add butter cubes and rub them into the flour with your fingers until the mixture resembles fine breadcrumbs.
3. Add water, one tablespoon at a time. Mix until it forms a soft dough.
4. Refrigerate for two hours before using.

Constructing the Pies:
1. Roll out the dough until it is ½ inch thick.
2. Cut 8 disks from the pastry.
3. Using a cup as a mold, pull the pastry up, overlapping the edges to create the free-standing pies.
4. Divide mincemeat among the pies.
5. Roll remaining pastry and cut 8 more discs for the lids.
6. Place lids on pies, pinching the pastry together to prevent leakage.
7. Use a knife to cut a cross on top to allow steam to escape.
8. Brush with the milk and sugar mix.
9. Bake for 20 minutes at 400°F.

Mince pies have a long and rich history in English holiday cooking. Its origins can be traced back to the 13th Century when Crusaders, returning home from the Holy Land, brought with them Middle Eastern recipes containing meats, fruits, and spices (yes, mincemeat was originally meat!). Many of the spices used were associated with the gifts delivered by the Magi to baby Jesus, and the pies were oblong, shaped like a manger.

Over the years, these pies were seen as Catholic "idolatry" and were cast out by many Protestants during the English Civil War. Despite this setback, the tradition of the Christmas pies continued well into the Victorian-Era, though by this time they were much sweeter, the meat was replaced with nothing but fruit, and their size had reduced immensely.

Today, the mince pie is still a popular treat in England, Ireland, and much of the English-speaking world (even haunted manor houses where organs mysteriously play at night).

The Doll's Ghost
By: F. Marion Crawford
1894

It was a terrible accident, and for a single moment, the grand house of Cranston Hall stood still. The butler emerged from the parlor where he rested, two grooms of the chambers entered the room from opposite directions, housemaids appeared on the grand staircase, and many say even Mrs. Pringle (the housekeeper) stood on the landing. The head nurse, the under nurse, and the nursery maid all watched in horror.

Lady Gwendolen Lancaster-Douglas-Scroop, the youngest daughter of the ninth Duke of Cranston, aged six years and three months, picked herself up and sat down on the third step from the foot of the grand staircase in Cranston House.

"Oh!" the butler cried out as he disappeared once again.

"Ah," responded the grooms as they went on their way.

"It's only that doll," Mrs. Pringle muttered.

The under nurse heard her say it. Then the three nurses gathered around Lady Gwendolen and patted her, offered her treats from their pockets, and hurried her out of Cranston House as fast as they could before someone found out that they had allowed their charge to tumble down the grand staircase with her doll in her arms. As the doll was badly broken, the nursery maid carried it, with the pieces all wrapped up in Lady Gwendolen's cloak. It was not far to Hyde Park, and when they found a quiet place, they stopped to make certain that Lady Gwendolen had no bruises, for the carpet was very thick and soft upon the stairs.

Lady Gwendolen Lancaster-Douglas-Scroop sometimes yelled, but she never cried. It was because she had yelled that the nurse had allowed her to go downstairs alone with Nina, the doll, under one arm, while she steadied herself on the banister with her other hand. Unfortunately, she had marched down the steps upon the polished marble steps beyond the edge of the carpet. So, she had fallen, and Nina had come to an untimely demise.

When the nurses were quite sure that she was not hurt, they unwrapped the doll and looked at her. She had been a very beautiful doll, very large and fair, with real yellow hair and eyelids that would open and shut over very grown-up dark eyes. When you moved her right arm up and down, she said, "Pa-pa," and when you moved her left arm, she said, "Ma-ma."

"I heard her say 'Pa,' when she fell," the under nurse said, who had heard everything. "But she should have said, 'Pa-pa.'"

"That's because her arm went up when she hit the step," the head nurse said. "She'll say the other 'Pa' when I put it down again."

"Pa," Nina said as her right arm was pushed down, speaking through her broken face. It was cracked right across from the upper corner of the forehead with a hideous gash, through the nose and down to the little frilled collar of the pale green silk Mother Hubbard frock, and two little triangles of porcelain had fallen out.

"It's a wonder she can speak at all!" the under nurse said, surprised.

"You'll have to take her to Mr. Puckler," her superior ordered. "It's not far… you'd better go at once."

Lady Gwendolen was busy digging a hole in the ground with a twig and paid no attention to the nurses.

"What are you doing?" the nursery maid inquired, watching the girl.

"Nina is dead, so I'm digging her a grave," her ladyship replied thoughtfully.

"Oh, she'll come back to life," the nursery maid assured the child. "Don't worry."

The under nurse wrapped Nina up again and set off. Fortunately, a kind soldier with very long legs happened to be nearby—he offered to see the under nurse to Mr. Puckler's and back.

Mr. Bernard Puckler and his daughter lived in a little house in an alley, just off of a quiet street not far from Belgrave Square. He was the great doll doctor—he mended dolls of all sizes and ages, boy dolls and girl dolls, baby dolls in long clothes and grown-up dolls in fashionable gowns, talking dolls and silent dolls, those that shut their eyes when they lay down, and those whose eyes were shut by a wire. His daughter, Else, was just over twelve years old, but she was already very clever at mending dolls' clothes and doing their hair (which is harder than you might think, though the dolls do sit nice and still while it is being done).

Mr. Puckler had originally been a German, but he had left his nationality behind him when he arrived in London many years ago, like a great many foreigners. He still had one or two German friends who came on Saturday evenings, smoked with him, and gambled with a few farthings. They even called him "Herr Doctor," which seemed to please Mr. Puckler very much.

He looked older than he was, for his beard was rather long and ragged, his hair was thin, and he wore horn-rimmed spectacles. As for Else, she was a thin, pale child, very quiet and neat, with dark eyes and brown hair that was pulled back in a braid and tied with a black ribbon. She was the one that took the dolls back to their homes when they were healthy and strong once again.

The house was a little one, but too big for the two people who lived in it. There was a small sitting room on the street, and the workshop was in the back, and there were three rooms upstairs. But the father and daughter spent most of their time in the workshop because they were always working, even in the evenings.

Mr. Puckler laid Nina on the table and looked at her for a long time, till the tears began to fill his eyes behind his spectacles. He was a very sensitive man and often fell in love with the dolls he mended. They were real little people to him, with personalities, thoughts, and feelings of their own, and he was tender with them all. But he fell in love at first sight with some of them, and when they were brought to him maimed and injured, they seemed so pitiful that he couldn't help but cry. You must remember that he grew up surrounded by dolls, and he understood them.

"How do you know that they don't feel anything?" he said to Else. "You must be gentle with them. It costs nothing to be kind to the little beings, and perhaps it makes a difference to them."

He fell instantly in love with Nina, perhaps because her beautiful brown glass eyes were similar to Else's, and he loved Else most of all, with all his heart. It was clear to Puckler that Nina had not been in the world for very long—her complexion was perfect, her hair was smooth where it should be smooth and curly where it should be curly, and her silk clothes were perfect. But across her face was the frightful gash, like a knife wound, deep and dark within but clean and sharp at the edges. When he tenderly pressed her head to close the gaping wound, the edges of the porcelain made a fine grating sound that was painful to hear, and the lids of the dark eyes quivered and trembled as if Nina was suffering.

"Poor Nina!" he exclaimed sorrowfully. "I promise I won't hurt you too much, though you will take a long time to heal."

He always asked the names of the broken dolls when they were brought to him. He liked "Nina" for a name. In every way, she pleased him more than any doll he had seen for many years, and he felt drawn to her. He quickly made up his mind to make her perfect and sound, no matter how much work it might be.

Mr. Puckler worked patiently a little at a time, and Else watched him. She could do nothing for poor Nina, whose clothes didn't need mending. The longer the doll doctor worked, the more fond he became of the yellow hair and the beautiful brown glass eyes. He sometimes forgot about the other dolls waiting to be fixed, lying side by side on the shelf. Sometimes, he sat for an hour gazing at Nina's face while he tried to come up with the perfect way to hide even the smallest trace of the terrible accident.

She was wonderfully mended—even Puckler had to admit it—but the scar was still visible to his keen eyes. It was a very fine line right across the face, downwards from right to left. Of course, there wasn't much else he could do—everything had gone right: the cement had set perfectly on the first try, and the weather had been fine and dry (which makes a great difference in a dolls' hospital).

At last, he knew that he could do no more, and the under nurse had already come twice to see whether the job was finished.

"Nina is not quite strong yet," Mr. Puckler had answered each time, for he could not say goodbye to the doll just yet.

And now he sat at the table where he worked, and Nina lay before him for the last time with a big brown box beside her. It stood there like her coffin, just waiting for her. He must put her into it and lay tissue paper over her dear face, and then put on the lid, and at the thought of tying the strings, his sight blurred with tears again. He was never going to look into the glassy depths of the beautiful brown eyes again, nor hear her little voice say, "Pa-pa," and "Mama." It was a painful moment for the man.

In the vain hope of gaining more time before the separation, he picked up the little sticky bottles of cement, glue, gum, and color, looking at each one before glancing up at Nina's face. All his small tools lay there, neatly arranged in a row, but he knew that he could not use them again for Nina. She was quite strong at last, and in a world where there were no cruel children to hurt her, she might live a hundred years, with only that almost invisible line across her face to tell of the fearful thing that had happened to her on the marble steps of Cranston House.

Suddenly Mr. Puckler's heart was quite full, and he jumped up from his seat and turned away.

"Else," he said, his voice shaking. "You must do it for me. I cannot bear to see her go into that box."

He moved to stand at the window with his back turned while Else did what he could not.

"Is it done?" he asked without turning around. "Then take her away, my dear. Put on your hat and take her to Cranston House quickly. I will turn around once you're gone."

Else was used to her father's peculiar ways with the dolls, and though she had never seen him so moved by a parting, she was not at all surprised.

"Come back quickly," he called out to her once she was at the door. "It's already getting late. I shouldn't send you out at this hour, but I cannot bear to go myself."

When Else was gone, he left the window and sat down in his place before the table again to wait for the child to come back. He touched the place where Nina had lain, very gently, and he recalled the softly tinted pink face, the glass eyes, and the ringlets of yellow hair until he could almost see them.

The evenings were long, and it was beginning to grow dark. Mr. Puckler wondered why Else did not come back. She had been gone an hour and a half, and that was much longer than he had expected, for it was barely half a mile from Belgrave Square to Cranston House. He convinced himself that the child might have been kept waiting, but as the twilight darkened, he grew anxious and began pacing in the dim workshop, no longer thinking of Nina but of Else, his own living child whom he loved.

An undefinable, unnerving sensation came upon him, a chilliness and a faint stirring of his thin hair, joined with a wish to be in any company rather than to be alone much longer. It was the beginning of fear.

He told himself in strong German-English that he was a foolish old man, and he began to search for matches. He knew just where they should be—for he always kept them in the same place: close to the little tin box that held bits of sealing wax of various colors. But somehow, he could not find the matches in the gloom.

Something had happened to Else, he was sure, and as his fear intensified, he believed he might calm down if he could light the room and see what time it was. Then he called himself a foolish old man again, and the sound of his own voice startled him in the dark. Where were those matches?

The window was gray still—he might see what time it was if he went close to it. He stood up from the table, pushed his chair in, and began to cross the floorboards.

Something was following him in the dark. There was a small pattering, much like tiny feet upon the boards. He stopped and listened, and the roots of his hair tingled. It was nothing, and he was just a foolish old man. He took two more steps, and he was sure that he heard the little pattering again. He turned his back to the window and faced the darkness. Everything was quiet and still, and it smelt of paste and cement and wood-fillings as usual.

"Is that you, Else?" he asked. He was surprised by the fear in his voice.

There was no answer in the room. He held up his watch to try to make out what time it was by the gray dusk that was not quite darkness yet. As far as he could see, it was within a few minutes of ten o'clock. He had been alone for a long time. He was so frightened for Else, who was out in London, so late, he nearly ran across the room to the door. As he fumbled for the latch, he distinctly heard the running of little feet after him.

"Mice," he muttered to himself as he finally managed to get the door open.

He shut it quickly behind him and felt as though some cold thing had settled onto his back and was clinging to him. The hall was quite dark, but he found his hat and was out in the alley in a moment's time, breathing more freely, and surprised to find how much light there still was in the open air. He could see the pavement clearly under his feet, and far off down the street, he could hear the laughter and calls of children playing a game. He wondered how he could have been so nervous, and for an instant, he thought of going back into the house to wait quietly for Else. But instantly, he felt that nervous fright of something washing over him again. In any case, it was better to walk to Cranston House and ask the servants about his child. Perhaps one of the women had taken a fancy to her and was giving her tea and cake.

He walked quickly to Belgrave Square and then up the broad streets, listening as we went for the tiny footsteps behind him. But he heard nothing and was laughing at himself when he rang the servants' bell at the big house. Of course, the child must be here.

The person who opened the door stared at Mr. Puckler, confused.

No little girl had been seen, and he knew "nothing about no dolls."

"She is my little girl," Mr. Puckler explained, trembling, for all of his anxiety was returning tenfold. "I am afraid something has happened to her."

The servant said rudely, "Nothing could have happened to her in this house because she hasn't been here. A jolly good thing too."

Mr. Puckler insisted on coming inside, for he wished to speak to the under nurse who knew him. But the man was ruder than ever and finally shut the door in his face.

When the doll doctor was alone on the street, he steadied himself with the railing. He felt as though he were breaking in two, just as some dolls break, in the middle of his chest.

Presently, he knew that he must do something to find Else, and that gave him strength. He began to walk as quickly as he could through the streets, following every highway and byway which his little girl might have taken on her errand. He asked several police officers in vain if they had seen her. Most of them answered him kindly, for they saw that he was sober and in his right mind, and some of them had little girls of their own.

It was one o'clock in the morning when he went up to his own door again, worn out, hopeless, and broken-hearted. As he turned the key in the lock, his heart stood still, for he knew that he was awake and not dreaming as he heard those tiny footsteps pattering to meet him from inside the house along the passage.

But he was too upset to be frightened anymore. His heart went on beating with a dull pain that found its way through him with every pulse. So he went in, hung up his hat in the dark, and found the matches in the cupboard and the candlestick in its place in the corner.

Mr. Puckler was so overcome and completely worn out that he sat down in his chair before the work table and nearly fainted as his face dropped forward upon his hands. Beside him, the solitary candle burned steadily with a low flame in the still-warm air.

"Else! Else!" he moaned against his knuckles. And that was all he could say, yet it was no relief to him. On the contrary—the very sound of her name was a new, sharp pain that pierced his ears and his head and his very soul. For every time he repeated the name, it meant that little Else was dead, somewhere out in the streets of London in the dark.

He was so terribly upset that he did not even feel something pulling gently at the hem of his old coat, so gently that it was like the nibbling of a tiny mouse. He might have thought that it really was a mouse had he noticed it.

"Else! Else!" he groaned against his hands.

Then a cool breath stirred his thin hair, and the low flame of the candle dropped down to a mere spark, not flickering as though a draft was going to blow it out, but just dropping down as if it had burned out on its own. Mr. Puckler felt his hands stiffen with fright, and there was a faint rustling sound, like some small bit of silk blowing in a gentle breeze. He sat up straight, stark and scared, and a small wooden voice spoke in the stillness.

"Pa-pa," it said with a break between the syllables.

Mr. Puckler jumped up, and his chair fell over with a smashing noise upon the wooden floor. The candle had almost gone out.

It was Nina's doll voice that had spoken—he would have known it among the voices of a hundred other dolls. And yet, there was something more to it… a little human ring with a pitiful cry and a call for help and possibly the wail of a hurt child. Mr. Puckler tried to look around, but he seemed to be frozen from head to foot.

Then, with a great effort, he raised one hand to each of his temples and pressed his own head around as he would have turned a doll's head. The candle was burning so low that it might as well have been out altogether, for any light it gave was null, and the room seemed quite dark. Then he saw something. He would not have believed that he could be more frightened than he had just been a moment before. But he was, and his knees shook, for he saw the doll standing in the middle of the floor, shining with a faint and ghostly radiance, her beautiful glassy brown eyes fixed on his. And across her face, the very thin line of the break that he had mended shone as though it were drawn in light with a fine point of a white flame.

Yet there was something more in the eyes too... there was something human. They were like Else's own, but as if only the doll saw him through those eyes, and not Else. Just seeing Else's eyes in the doll's face was enough to bring back all his pain and to make him forget his fear.

"Else! My little Else!" he cried out loud.

The small ghost moved, and its doll-arm slowly rose and fell with a stiff, mechanical motion.

"Pa-pa," it said.

It seemed this time that there was even more of Else's voice, echoing somewhere between the wooden notes that reached his ears so distinctly and yet so far away. Else was calling him, he was sure of it.

His face was white in the gloom, but his knees did not shake anymore, and he felt that he was less frightened.

"Yes, child, I'm here! But where?" he asked. "Where are you, Else?"

"Pa-pa!"

The syllables died away in the quiet room. There was a low rustling of silk, the glassy brown eyes turned slowly away, and Mr. Puckler heard the pitter-patter of the small feet in the bronze slippers as the figure ran straight to the door. Then the candle burned high again, the room was full of light, and he was alone.

Mr. Puckler passed his hand over his eyes and looked around. He could see everything quite clearly, and he felt that he must have been dreaming, though he was standing instead of sitting down as he should have been if he had just woken up. The candle burned brightly now. There were the dolls to be mended, lying in a row. The third one had lost her right shoe, and Else was making a new one. He knew that, and he was certainly not dreaming now. He had not been dreaming when he had come in from his fruitless search and had heard the doll's footsteps running to the door. He had not fallen asleep in his chair. How could he possibly have fallen asleep when his heart was breaking? He had been awake the entire time.

He steadied himself, picked up the fallen chair and set it upon its legs, and said to himself once again that he was a foolish old man. He should be out in the streets looking for his child, asking questions, talking to the police, visiting the hospitals.

"Pa-pa!"

The longing, wailing, pitiful little wooden cry rang from the passage outside the door, and Mr. Puckler stood for an instant with a white face, transfixed and rooted to the spot. A moment later, his hand was on the latch. Then he was in the passage, with the light streaming from the open door behind him.

At the other end of the hall, he saw the little phantom shining clearly in the darkness, and the right hand seemed to beckon him as the arm rose and fell once more. He knew all at once that it had not come to frighten him but to lead him, and when it disappeared, and he walked boldly toward the door, he knew that it was in the street outside, waiting for him. He forgot that he was tired and that he had not eaten supper—for a sudden hope ran through him, like a golden stream of life.

Sure enough, at the corner of the alley and at the corner of the street and out in Belgrave Square, he saw the small ghost flitting before him. Sometimes it was only a shadow, the glare from the lamps casting a pale green sheen on its little Mother Hubbard frock of silk, and sometimes where the streets were dark and silent, the whole figure shone brightly with its yellow curls and rosy cheeks. It seemed to trot along like a tiny child, and Mr. Puckler could almost hear the pattering of the slippers on the pavement as it ran. But it moved so quickly, and he could only just keep up with it, tearing along with his hat on the back of his head and his thin hair blowing in the night breeze.

On and on he went, and he had no idea where he was. He did not even care, for he knew with certainty that he was going the right way.

Then, at last, in a wide, quiet street, he was standing before a large door with two lamps on each side of it and a polished brass bell handle he pulled.

Just inside, when the door was opened, in the bright light, there was the little shadow and the pale green sheen of the little silk dress, and once more, the small cry came to his ears, less pitiful this time and more longing.

"Pa-pa!"

The shadow turned suddenly bright, and out of the brightness, the beautiful brown glass eyes were turned up happily to his, while the rosy mouth smiled so divinely that the phantom doll looked almost like a little angel.

"A little girl was brought in soon after ten o'clock," said the hushed voice of the hospital doorkeeper. "I think they thought she was only stunned. She was holding a big brown box with her, and they could not get it out of her hands. Her hair was brown and pulled back into a long braid."

"She is my little girl," Mr. Puckler said, but he barely heard his own voice.

He leaned over Else's face in the gentle light of the children's ward, and when he had stood there a minute, the beautiful brown eyes opened and looked up to his.

"Papa!" Else cried softly. "I knew you would come!"

Then Mr. Puckler did not know what he did or said for a moment. What he felt was worth all the fear and terror and despair that had almost killed him that night. By and by, Else told her story:

"They were big boys with bad faces," Else said. "And they tried to get Nina away from me, but I held on tight and fought as much as I could till one of them hit me with something. I don't remember any more, but I think I fell. I suppose the boys ran away and somebody found me there. But I'm afraid Nina is all smashed."

"Here is the box," the nurse whispered softly as there were two other children in the room, sound asleep. "We could not take it out of her arms until she woke up. Would you like to see if the doll is broken?"

She untied the string very quickly, but Nina was all smashed to pieces. Only the gentle light of the children's ward made a pale green sheen on the folds of the little Mother Hubbard frock.

The Lover's Farewell
By: Catherine Crowe
1859

"But there are no ghosts now," objected Mr. R.

"Quite the contrary," I said. "I'm confident that everyone in this circle has either had an experience or was a confidant of a friend's experience."

After some discussion on the existence of ghosts, it was agreed that each should relate a story—but we all agreed to tell a true story where the circumstances either happened to ourselves or had been told to us by someone who was confident in their experience.

We followed the order in which we were sitting around the fire, and Miss P began:

"Some years ago, I was engaged to be married to an officer. But, unfortunately, circumstances prevented the union from happening as early as we had hoped. Meanwhile, Captain S, whose regiment was in the West Indies, was ordered to join. I don't think I need to tell you that this separation upset us a great deal. We consoled each other as best as we could by writing letters. But, of course, letters took much longer, and their arrival was never guaranteed as they are today. Still, I heard regularly from him and had no reason for any uneasiness.

"One day, I had been out shopping and returned home rather tired. I told my mother that I was going to go lie down for an hour before we went out that evening. I went to my room, pulled a book off the shelf, and threw myself on the bed to read before dozing off. I had read a page or two, and feeling drowsy, I laid the book down and fell asleep. I must not have been asleep for very long when there was a knock at my chamber door.

"'Come in,' I said without turning my head, for I thought it was the maid coming to fetch my dress that I was going to wear that evening.

"I heard the door open, and a person entered, but it wasn't the maid. I looked around and saw that it was Captain S. I can't tell you what came over me. I knew very little of mesmerism at the time. Still, I have since thought that when a spirit appears, it must have some power of mesmerizing the spectator—I've heard other people in similar situations describe what I went through myself. I was perfectly calm, not the least bit frightened or surprised, but I was transfixed. Of course, had I been in a normal state, I would have either been amazed at seeing Captain S so unexpectedly (especially in my chamber!), or if I believed it was an apparition, I would have been alarmed. But I was neither. I can't say whether I thought it was him or his ghost. It seemed as if my mind simply accepted the phenomenon without question.

"Captain S approached the bedside and spoke to me just as he always did, and I answered him in the same manner. After the first greeting, he crossed the room to fetch a chair. He wore his uniform, and when his back was turned, I remember distinctly seeing the seams of his coat. He brought the chair over from the dressing table, and sitting at my bedside, we talked for about half an hour. Then, he rose and, looking at his watch, said his time was up and he had to go. He said goodbye and went out the same door he had entered.

"The moment it closed behind him, I knew what had happened. His power over me vanished when he disappeared, and I returned to my normal state. I screamed and seized the bell rope which I rang with such violence, I broke it. My mother, who was in the room underneath, rushed up the stairs, followed by the servants. They found me on the floor, fainted, and I was unable to speak for some time. Once I calmed down, I asked the servants to leave the room and then told my mother what had happened. Of course, she thought it was a dream, but I assured her that it was not. I even pointed to the chair which had actually been brought to the bedside by the spirit—there it stood exactly as he had placed it.

"'You know where that chair usually is,' I argued. 'When you were up here a little while ago, it was in its usual place—as it was when I laid down. I never moved it. It was placed there by Captain S.'

"My mother was perplexed. I was so confident, and yet she believed the whole ordeal to be impossible.

"From that moment on, I only thought of Captain S as one departed from this life. I was certain of it, and I was spared of all the suspense and agonies of a pining fiancée.

"Accordingly, about a month later, Major B of my beloved's regiment sent his card, and I said to my mother, 'Now you'll see. He's coming to tell me of Henry's death.'

"And so it was. Captain S had died of a fever on the day he paid me that mysterious visit."

We asked Miss P if any similar circumstances had ever occurred to her before or since.

"Never," she answered. "I never saw anything of the sort but on that one occasion."

Oyster Stew

Inspired by a Recipe from 1896

Ingredients:
1 onion, minced
1 clove of garlic, minced
1 large potato, chopped
4 tbsp of butter
3 cups of milk
1 cup of heavy cream
2 12 oz jars of oysters, chopped (save the liquor)
Salt and pepper to taste
Tobasco (optional)

Directions:
1. Sauté the onion and garlic in the butter over medium heat. Add the potato. Season with salt and pepper and sauté for 15 minutes.
2. Add milk and simmer until potatoes are cooked (approximately 20 minutes).
3. Add heavy cream, the oysters, and their liquor. The oysters are fully cooked when their edges curl.
4. Serve topped with Tobasco sauce (optional).

The tradition of eating oyster stew on Christmas Eve became popular in America when Irish immigrants arrived.

The vast majority of these new citizens were Catholic, and eating meat the night before a religious holiday was forbidden, so they brought their stew of milk, butter, pepper, and ling fish with them. Arriving in New York City, they replaced the fish with oysters which were readily available and enjoyed by everyone—the rich and the poor.

Oyster stew wasn't the only staple in the Victorian Christmas dinner—raw oysters in the shell and oyster stuffing were also popular dishes to pass. The popularity of oysters and oyster stew at Christmas has survived into the 21st Century and even appeared in literary works such as *The Age of Innocence* by Edith Wharton.

Between the Lights
By: E.F. Benson
1912

The snow had fallen incessantly from sunrise until the gradual shift of white light to darkness indicated that the sun had set again. But as usual, at the delightful home of Everard Chandler where I often spent Christmas (and was spending it now), there was constant entertainment, and we were shocked at how quickly the hours had passed. A billiard tournament filled the time between breakfast and lunch, followed by a huge game of hide-and-seek all over the house. Perhaps it was the enchantment of Christmas that had made us feel like children once again, tip-toeing up and down dimly lit passages, terrified a wild screaming form might dart out in front of us. Then, exhausted from the game, we assembled for tea in the hall, a room of shadows and panels on which the light from the wide-open fireplace which burned a divine mixture of peat and moss flickered and grew bight again. It was then that the proper Christmas tradition began.

As was proper, the electric lights were shut off so everyone could listen to the ghost stories and imagine anything lurking in the corners of the room. We entertained one another with tales of blood, bones, skeletons, armor, and shrieks.

I had just added my contribution to the ghostly tale, confident that I had spun the worst tale yet, when Everard, who had not yet shared a story, spoke. He was sitting across from me in the full blaze of the fire, still pale and delicate after recovering from an illness in the fall. All the same, he managed to keep up with everyone while exploring the darkest places of the house, and the look on his face now startled me.

"I don't mind that sort of thing," he declared. "I can't help but feel as if ghosts have become a bit trite. When I hear stories of mysterious screams and skeletons, I feel like I'm in familiar territory, and all I need to do is hide under my blankets."

"But the blankets were just twitched away by my skeleton," I defended my tale.

"I didn't even remember that. Why, I believe there are seven or eight skeletons in this room now, covered with blood and skin and other horrors. No…" his voice trailed off for a moment. "The nightmares of our childhood were truly frightening. They were vague. There was a true horror about them because we didn't know what we feared. Now, if someone could recapture that—"

Mrs. Chandler got quickly out of her seat.

"Oh, Everard," she sighed. "Surely you don't want to recapture that. Once was enough."

We were all captivated by their mysterious exchange. A chorus of invitation asked him to proceed: a true first-hand ghost story (which was what seemed to be indicated) was too precious a thing for us to lose.

Everard laughed. "No, my dear. I don't want to recapture it again at all," he said to his wife before turning to look at the rest of us. "In truth, I suppose it was just a nightmare. There was not much to see, and you'll probably say that it was nothing and wonder why I was frightened. But I was. It frightened me out of my wits. But I know I saw something… though I can't say what it was."

"It doesn't matter," I said. "Tell us about it."

There was a stir of movement about the circle around the fire… and not all physical. It was as if—this is only what I personally felt—it was as if the childish gaiety of the hours we had passed playing died instantly. Now there was to be real hide-and-seek—real terrors were going to be lurking in the dark.

"Oh, Everard," Mrs. Chandler cried out as she sat back down. "Won't this upset you?"

It didn't matter—it was upsetting the rest of us.

The room remained in dubious darkness except for the sudden light along the walls by the leaping flames on the hearth, and there were endless possibilities as to what might lurk in the dim corners of the room. Moreover, Everard, who had been sitting in bright light before, was now banished into the shadows by an extinguished log. A voice alone spoke to us as he sat back in his chair.

"Last year," he began slowly, "on December 24th, we were down here, as usual—Amy and I—for Christmas. Several of you who are here now were here then. Three or four of you at least."

I was one of these, but like the others, I stayed silent. Everard went on without pausing.

"Those of you who were here then will remember how very warm it was on this day last year. You will remember too that we played croquet that day on the lawn. It was perhaps a little cold for croquet, and we played it to simply be able to say that we did it. Much more enjoyable than today. I wouldn't be surprised if there were three feet of snow outside. More, probably. Listen."

A sudden draft flew from the chimney, and the fire flared up. The wind drove the snow against the windows, making us all huddle closer to the fire. As we sat and listened, we heard the soft scurry of the falling flakes against the panes, like the soft tread of dozens of little people who stepped lightly. Hundreds of little feet seemed to be gathering outside; only the glass kept them out. Of the imaginary skeletons present, I was sure four or five turned to look at the windows. Nervous, I glanced over my shoulder to gaze at the nearest window myself. They were small-paned with leaden bars. Little heaps of snow had gathered on the leaden bars, but there was nothing else to be seen.

"Yes, last Christmas Eve was very warm and sunny," Everard went on. "We had had no frost that autumn, and our dahlias were still in bloom. I always thought it must have been mad... and perhaps I was mad too."

No one interrupted him.

I heard Mrs. Chandler stir in her chair.

Never had there been such a cheerful party reduced to complete silence within five minutes. Instead of laughing at ourselves for playing silly games, we were all taking a serious game far too seriously.

"Anyway, I was sitting out while you," he turned to me, "and my wife played your round of croquet. Then it struck me that perhaps it wasn't as warm as I had thought because quite suddenly, I shivered. I looked up, but I did not see either of you playing croquet at all. I saw something which had no relation to you or her… at least I hope not."

Now the angler lands his fish, the stalker spots his stag, and the speaker holds his audience.

And as the fish is gaffed, and as the stag is shot, so were we held. There was no getting away till he had finished with us.

"You all know the croquet lawn," Everard continued, "and how it is surrounded by a flower border with a brick wall behind it, and there is only one gate.

"Well, I looked up and saw that the lawn—I could barely see that it was still the lawn—was shrinking, and the walls were closing in on it. As the walls closed in, they grew higher. At the same time, the light began to fade from the sky till it grew quite dark, and only a glimmer of light came through the gate.

"There was, as I told you, a dahlia in bloom that day, and as this awful darkness and confusion washed over me, I remember staring at it, desperate for anything familiar. But it was no longer a dahlia, and its red petals were the red of some dim firelight. It was then that the hallucination was complete. I was no longer sitting on the lawn watching croquet, but rather in a low-roofed room... something like a cattle shed, but round. Close above my head, even though I was sitting down, ran rafters from wall to wall. It was nearly dark though a bit of light came in from the door opposite me, which seemed to lead down a passage. It was an oppressive, foul place—stuffy, crowded, and dense. It was as if this place had been the place of some sort of human menagerie, a dreadful den. Yet, the oppressiveness was nothing compared to the horror of the place from the view of the spirit. The sense of crime and abomination to men and women who were treated more like animals than humans hung heavy in the air. In addition, there was a sense of the weight of the years... as if I had been thrown back in time."

He paused for a moment, and the fire on the hearth leaped up for a second and then died down again. But in that gleam, I saw that all the faces were turned to Everard and that all wore some look of dread. Certainly, I felt it myself and waited in horror for what was coming.

"As I told you," he continued, "where the dahlia had been now burned a dim fire, and my eyes were drawn there. Shapes were gathered around it though I could not make them out at first. Perhaps my eyes became more accustomed to the dark, or the fire burned brighter because I could see them eventually. They were of human form but very small, for when one rose to his feet with a horrible chattering, his head was still a few inches from the low roof. He was dressed in a shirt that came to his knees, and his arms were bare and covered with hair.

"Then the chattering increased, and I knew that they were talking about me, for they kept pointing at me. At that, my horror grew, for I became suddenly aware that I was powerless and could not move my hands or feet—no doubt this nightmare had possession over me. In the paralysis of my fear, I tried to scream, but I couldn't utter a sound.

"All this took place in the instant of a dream, for all at once and without any transition, the whole thing had vanished, and I was back on the lawn where my wife was still aiming for her stroke. But my face was sweating, and I was trembling all over.

"Now, you may all say that I had fallen asleep and simply had a nightmare. That may be so... but I wasn't sleepy before, nor was I sleepy afterward. It was as if someone had held a book before me, whisked the pages open for a second, and then slammed it shut once more."

Somebody (I don't know who) got up from his chair so suddenly, it made me jump and turned on the electric light. I do not mind confessing that I was relieved of this.

Everard laughed. "Shall I go on?"

I don't think anyone replied, but he went on.

"Well, let us say that it wasn't a dream, but rather a hallucination. Whichever it was, it haunted me for months. It was never quite out of my mind, always lingered somewhere in the corners of my mind, sometimes sleeping quietly and other times stirring awake. It was no use telling myself that it had never happened, for it felt as if something had entered my very soul—like a seed of horror had been planted there. As the weeks passed, the seed began to sprout. I won't say it affected my health, though I know I wasn't eating or sleeping.

"Often, while I was eating or drinking, I would pause and wonder if it was all worthwhile.

"Eventually, I told two people, hoping that by talking about it, that might somehow help matters. I told my wife, who laughed at me, and my doctor, who also laughed at me and assured me I was in perfect health. He encouraged us to travel to keep my mind off things and declared that he would stake his reputation on the certainty that I was not going mad.

"While in Scotland, we stayed in a place called Glen Callan, very remote and wild near the sea. I was told to always bring my compass with me in case a thick sea-mist ventured inland. Of course, over the weeks, the weather was always bright and clear, and one day, I left home without it.

"I hiked nearly six miles to a part of the property that I had never been to before, down a steep hill to a loch. The morning had been extraordinarily warm with a little wind blowing off the sea. Since arriving in Scotland, I had felt an extreme sense of peace. Not once since Christmas had I been so free of fear, and I smiled as I lay looking up at the blue sky, watching my smoke-whorls from my pipe curl away into nothingness. But I was not allowed to relax for long. My companion said that the weather had changed and the wind had shifted again, and we should get back on the path as soon as possible. He feared a sea-mist would come in.

"'This is a bad place to get stuck in the mist,' he added, nodding toward the crags we had climbed along the loch.

"Strangely, he insisted on going back down over the rocks and boulders when there was a perfectly nice path that led back to the lodge. He offered excuse after excuse—there were mossy patches (untrue as summer had been nothing but warm and sunny), it was a longer path and would take too long (also obviously untrue), there were so many snakes. But none of his arguments convinced me, so at last, he gave in and followed me down the path.

"We weren't even halfway down the hill when the mist surrounded us. In less than three minutes, we were enveloped in a cloud of fog so thick that we could barely see a dozen yards in front of us. I was relieved we weren't clambering down those crags and confident of my sense of direction, despite having left my compass at home. More than anything, the complete freedom from fear was euphoric—I hadn't known pure joy since Christmas, and I felt as giddy as a schoolboy home for the holidays. But the mist grew thicker and thicker, and I was getting soaked—the wetness seeped through my clothes to my skin and chilled my very bones. And still, it felt as if we were making no headway even after an hour.

"Behind me, my companion muttered to himself, but he stayed close to me as if he was afraid.

"Now, there are many unpleasant companions in this world. I would not want to be on that misty path with a drunk man or a maniac. But worse than either of those things, I think is a frightened man. His fear is infectious and impossible to ignore. I began to be afraid too.

"From there, it is easy to let the fear take over you. Other peculiar things began to happen too. At one moment, we seemed to be walking on flat ground, and at another, I felt sure we were climbing again while all the time we should have been descending. Unless, of course, we were lost. Also, it was October, so it was beginning to get dark, but I was relieved when I remembered that the full moon would rise soon after sunset. But it had grown so cold, and instead of rain, we were walking through a steady fall of snow.

"Things were pretty bad, but then for an instant, we seemed to be saved when I heard to my left the sound of the river that ran from the loch to our lodge. It should have been straight in front of me, and we were perhaps a mile out of our way, but this was better than the blind wandering of the last hour. Turning to the left, I marched toward the river. But before I had gone a hundred yards, I heard a sudden choked cry behind me and turned to see my companion flee in terror, disappearing into the mist. I called after him but heard nothing but the sound of his footsteps disappearing into the distance.

"I didn't know what had frightened him, but with him and his fear gone, I managed to forget my own fears and continued on, almost relieved to be alone. That relief vanished the minute I saw a deep, dark blackness in front of me. Before I knew what I was doing, I was stumbling up a very steep grassy slope.

"During the last few minutes, the wind had picked up, and the snow whipped around me violently. As I hesitated on this slope, I became aware of two things: one, the blackness in front of me was suddenly closer, and the other, whatever this thing was, sheltered me from the snow. I shivered as the snow bit away at my cheeks and decided to venture a few steps into the blackness's shelter. It was better than freezing to death.

"A wall about twelve feet high appeared, and right where I bumped into it, there was a hole—a door. I could see a bit of light appearing around it. Feeling the winter chill on my back, I pushed the door open and bent down to make my way through the low passage before coming out on the other side.

"I was in a circular room with a low ceiling. As I looked around, I noticed that there were broken stones supporting a floor above me. Then two things happened at the same time:

"The terror I had felt over the last nine months came rushing back to me, and it was as if the vision I had seen in the garden was finally fulfilled. At the same moment of this realization, I saw a little man running toward me, but only about three feet tall. I saw the man. I heard him stumble over a stone. I smelled something foul. And my soul told me that something was wrong… very wrong. I think I tried to scream, but I could not. I tried to move but could not. The tiny creature crept closer.

"Then I suppose the terror which had held me captivated for so long spurred me to move. The next moment I heard myself screaming as I stumbled through the passage. I leaped down the grassy slope and ran faster than I ever hope to run again. I don't know which way I ran, nor did I care so long as I put distance between myself and that place. Luck favored me, and after an hour, I reached the lodge.

"Next day, I felt a chill, and as you know, I was sick with pneumonia for six weeks.

"Well, that is my story, and there are many explanations. You may say that I fell asleep on the lawn and again on the hill overlooking the loch. There are hundreds of ways to explain it. But the coincidence was an odd one. Those who believe in spirits or the second sight might look into it a bit more."

"And that is all?" I asked.

"Yes, that is all. In fact, it was nearly too much for me. And with that, I think it's time for bed."

The Ghost's Summons
By: Ada Buisson
1868

"Wanted, sir—a patient."

It was in the early days of my professional career when patients were scarce, and money was even scarcer. Even though I had just sat down with a glass of steaming punch in honor of the Christmas season, I jumped up and hurried to my surgery.

I entered briskly. But no sooner did I catch sight of the figure leaning against the counter than I stepped back with a strange feeling of horror that I could not comprehend for the life of me.

I shall never forget the ghastliness of that face—the white horror stamped upon every feature—the agony which seemed to sink the very eyes beneath the furrowed brow. It was awful to look at, even if I was accustomed to scenes of terror.

"You need assistance," I began slowly.

"No. I am not ill."

"You require then—"

"Hush!" he interrupted as he approached me, dropping his already low murmur to a mere whisper. "I believe you are not wealthy... Would you be willing to earn a thousand pounds?"

A thousand pounds! His words seemed to burn my very ears.

"I should like to if I could do so honestly," I replied, trying to maintain my dignity. "What is it you need done?"

A peculiar look of intense horror passed over the white face before me, but the blue-black lips answered firmly, "To attend a deathbed."

"A thousand pounds to attend a deathbed? Where am I to go then? Whose is it?"

"Mine."

The voice in which this was said sounded so hollow and distant that involuntarily I shrank back. "Yours!" I cried. "What nonsense! You are not a dying man. You are pale, but you appear perfectly healthy. You—"

"Hush!" he interrupted. "I know all this. You cannot be more convinced of my physical health than I am myself. Yet

I know that before the clock tolls the first hour after midnight, I shall be a dead man."

"But—"

He shuddered slightly. Stretching out his hand commandingly, he motioned me to be silent. "I know too much," he said quietly. "I have received a mysterious summons from the dead. No mortal can help me. I am as doomed as the wretch on whom the judge has already passed sentence. I do not come to seek your advice or to argue with you, but simply to buy your services. I offer you a thousand pounds to pass the night in my chamber and witness the scene that takes place. The sum may seem extravagant to you. But I have no further need for my money, and I'm sure the sight you'll be witness to will be a horrible one."

The words, strange as they were, were spoken calmly. But as the last sentence dropped slowly from those lips, an expression of such wild horror again passed over the stranger's face that, in spite of the small fortune offered to me, I hesitated to answer.

"You fear to trust the promise of a dead man. Look here," he exclaimed eagerly. In the blink of an eye, a piece of parchment appeared on the counter between us. I read the words, *And to Mr. Frederick Kead, of 14 High Street, Alton, I bequeath the sum of one thousand pounds for certain services rendered to me.*

"I have had that will drawn up within the last twenty-four hours, and I signed it an hour ago in the presence of competent witnesses. I am prepared, you see. Now, do you accept my offer or not?"

I didn't say a word. Instead, I walked across the room, took down my hat, and then locked the door of the surgery connected to the house.

It was a dark, icy cold night, and somehow the courage and determination which the sight of my own name in connection with a thousand pounds had given me dropped considerably as I found myself wandering through the silent darkness with a man whose deathbed I was about to attend.

He was a grim sight, and as his hand touched mine, in spite of the frost, it felt like a burning coal.

On we went—tramp, tramp through the snow—on and on till even I grew weary. At length, I heard the chimes of a church bell, and in the distance, I could make out the snowy hills of a churchyard.

Heavens! Was this awful scene to take place among the dead?

"Eleven," groaned the doomed man. "Gracious God! Only two more hours and that ghostly messenger will bring the summons. Come along, let's hurry!"

There was a short road separating us from a wall that surrounded a large mansion. We ran along the wall until we came to a small door.

Passing through this, in a few minutes, we were silently climbing the private staircase to a splendidly furnished apartment, which left no doubt to the wealth of its owner.

All was intensely silent throughout the house. But in this room, in particular, there was a stillness that, as I gazed around, unnerved me.

My companion glanced at the clock on the mantle and sank into a large chair by the side of the fire with a shudder. "Only an hour and a half longer," he muttered. "I thought I was braver than this." Then in a fiercer tone, clutching my arm, he added, "You mock me! You think I'm mad! But wait until you see… just wait!"

I put my hand on his wrist. There was now a fever in his sunken eyes, matching the superstitious chill I had felt. It made me hope that my initial suspicion was correct and that my patient was but the victim of some fearful hallucination.

"Mock you?" I tried to soothe the man. "Far from it. I sympathize with you and wish to help you. You must sleep. Lie down and let me keep watch."

He groaned but stood up and began throwing his clothes off. Seeing my opportunity, I slipped a sleeping powder (which I had managed to put into my pocket before leaving the surgery) into his wine glass on the table beside him.

The more I saw, the more convinced I was that my patient's nervous system required my attention. It was with sincere satisfaction I saw him drink the wine and then stretch himself on the luxurious bed.

Ha, I thought as the clock struck twelve, and instead of a groan, the deep breathing of the sleeping man sounded through the room. *You won't receive any summons tonight.*

Noiselessly, I replenished the fire, poured myself a large glass of wine, and drawing the curtain so that the firelight would not disturb my patient, I, too, laid down.

How long I slept, I do not know, but suddenly I woke with a start and as ghostly a thrill of horror as I have ever felt in my life.

Something—just what I did not know—seemed near, something nameless but unbelievably awful.

I gazed around.

The fire emitted a faint blue glow, just sufficient to see that the room was exactly the same as when I had fallen asleep. But I could see that the clock's long hand was just five minutes away from the mysterious hour which was to be the death-moment of the "summoned" man.

Was there any truth in the strange story he had told me?

The silence was intense.

I could not even hear a breath from the bed. I was about to rise and approach when again that awful horror seized me, and at that same moment, my eyes fell upon the mirror opposite the door, and I saw—

Good God in Heaven! That awful Shape—that ghastly mockery of what had been humanity—was it really a messenger from the buried, quiet dead?

It stood there in a death shroud, and the awful face had a pair of sunken eyes that gleamed forth a green glassy glare which seemed like a veritable blast from the infernal fires below.

To move or utter a sound in that hideous presence was impossible. Like a statue, I sat and saw that horrid Shape move slowly toward the bed.

I didn't know what happened—I heard nothing except for a low, stifled, agonized groan, and I saw the shadow of that ghastly messenger bending over the bed.

I'm not sure whether the Shape conveyed some dreadful but wordless sentence from its breathless lips, but for an instant, the shadow of a claw-like hand, from which the third finger was missing, extended over the doomed man's head. And then, as the clock struck one clear silvery stroke, it fell, and a wild shriek rang through the room—a death-shriek.

I don't usually faint, but I must confess that the next ten minutes, my existence was cold and blank. When I did manage to stagger to my feet, I gazed around, trying to understand the chilly horror which still possessed me.

Thank God that room was rid of that awful presence. Gulping down some wine, I lit a candle and staggered toward the bed. How I prayed that, after all, I might have been dreaming and that my own excited imagination had simply conjured up some hideous memory from the dissecting room.

But one glance was enough to dash those hopes.

No! The summons had indeed been given and answered.

I flashed the light over the dead face, swollen, still tense with the agony of death. I suddenly shrank back.

Even as I gazed, the expression of the face seemed to change: the blackness faded into a deathly whiteness, the tense features relaxed, and even as if the victim of that dreaded apparition still lived, a sad, solemn smile appeared across the pale lips.

I was intensely horrified, but I still retained enough self-consciousness to be struck professionally by such a phenomenon. Surely there was something more than the supernatural in all of this?

Again, I scrutinized the dead face and even the throat and chest. With the exception of a tiny pimple on one temple beneath a clump of hair, there wasn't a single mark on the body. To look at the corpse, one would have believed that this man had indeed died by the visitation of God, peacefully, while sleeping.

I don't know how long I stood there, but it was long enough to gather my scattered senses and to reflect that, all things considered, my own position would be very unpleasant if I was found in the room with a mysteriously dead man.

So, as noiselessly as I could, I made my way out of the house. No one met me on the private staircase. The little door opening onto the road was easily unlocked. I was thankful to feel, once again, the fresh wintry air as I hurried along the road by the churchyard.

Soon after, there was a magnificent funeral at that church. It was said that the young widow of the buried man was inconsolable. And then the rumors began to spread of a horrible apparition which had been seen on the night of the man's death. It was whispered that the young widow was terrified and insisted on leaving her splendid mansion.

I was too mystified with the whole affair to risk my reputation by saying what I knew, and I should have allowed my secrets to remain forever buried in oblivion. And I would have... if I had not suddenly heard that the widow, objecting to many of the legacies in the last will of her husband, intended to fight it on the grounds of insanity (for she had heard the rumor that he believed he had received a mysterious summons).

On this, I went to the lawyer and sent a message to the lady that, as the last person who had attended her husband, I could prove his sanity. I requested an interview where I hoped to share the strange and horrible story. The same evening, I received an invitation to go to the mansion. I was ushered immediately into a splendid room, and there, standing before the fire, was the most dazzlingly beautiful young creature I had ever seen.

She was very small but exquisite—had it not been for the way she carried herself, I would have believed she was a mere child. With a curtsy, she advanced but did not speak.

"I come on a strange and painful errand," I began but then stopped suddenly. I happened to glance full into her eyes and from them down to the small right hand grasping the chair. The wedding ring was on her right hand.

"I understand that you are Mr. Kead who requested to tell me some absurd ghost story and whom my late husband mentions here." As she spoke, she stretched out her left hand toward something—but what it was, I did not know, for my eyes were fixed on that hand.

The horror! White and delicate as it may be, it was shaped like a claw, and the third finger was missing!

One sentence was enough after that. "Madam, all I can tell you is that a singular deformity marked the ghost who summoned your husband. The third finger of the left hand was missing," I said sternly. The next instant, I had left that beautiful sinful presence.

The man's will was never disputed. The next morning, I received a check for a thousand pounds. The next bit of news I heard of the widow was that she had herself seen that awful apparition and had left the mansion immediately.

Hot Brandy and Rum Punch
Inspired by a Recipe from 1862

Ingredients:
1 qt of rum (dark)
1 qt of brandy
1 lb of sugar (cubes preferred)
4 lemons
3 qt of boiling water
1 tsp of nutmeg

Directions:
1. Rub the sugar cubes over the lemons until it has absorbed all the yellow of the skins, then place the sugar cubes in a (heat safe) punch bowl.
2. Pour in the boiling water. Stir well.
3. Add the rum, brandy, and nutmeg. Mix.

Horror: A True Tale

By: John Berwick Harwood
1861

I was only nineteen years of age when the incident occurred, which has thrown a shadow over my life. How many weary years have dragged on since then?

Young, happy, and beloved was I in those long-departed days. They said that I was beautiful. The mirror now reflects a haggard old woman with ashen lips and a pale face. But do not think that you are listening to a mere lament. It is not the flight of years that has brought me to this wreck of my former self: had it been so, I could have accepted the loss cheerfully and patiently as it happens to all of us. But it was no natural progress of decay which robbed me of my youth (and of the hopes and joys that belong to youth), snapped the link that bound my heart to another's, and doomed me to be alone in my old age.

I try to be patient, but my cross has been heavy, and my heart is empty and weary. I long for the death that comes so slowly to those who pray to die.

I will try to relate, exactly as it happened, the event which blighted my life. Though it occurred many years ago, there is no fear that I should have forgotten any of the minutest details: they were stamped on my brain too clearly, like the brand of a red-hot iron. I see them written in the wrinkles of my brow, in the dead whiteness of my hair, which was a glossy brown once—it knew no gradual change from dark to gray, from gray to white, as with those happy ones who were my childhood friends, whose honored age is soothed by the love of children and grandchildren.

But I must not envy them. I only meant to say that the difficulty of my task has no connection with not remembering—I remember it all too well. But as I take the pen, my hand trembles, my head swims, the old rushing faintness and horror comes over me again, and the well-remembered fear is upon me. Yet, I will go on.

This is my story:

I was a great heiress, I believe, though I cared little for the fact. My father had wealth and no son to inherit it. His three daughters (of whom I was the youngest) were to share the acres of land among them. I have said, and truly that I cared little for this. Indeed, I was so rich then in health, youth, and love, that I felt myself quite indifferent to all else. The possession of all the treasures of earth could never have made up for what I then had… and lost.

Of course, we girls knew that we were heiresses, but I do not think Lucy and Minnie were any prouder or happier because of it. I know I was not. Reginald did not court me for my money. Of *that,* I was quite certain. He proved that when he shrank from my side after the change. Yes, in all my lonely age, I can still be thankful that he did not keep his word (as some would have done), did not clasp my hand at the altar—a hand he had learned to loathe and shudder at—simply because it was full of gold. At least he spared me that.

I know that I was loved and that knowledge has kept me from going mad through many a weary day and restless night, when my hot eyeballs had not a tear to shed and even to weep was a luxury denied to me.

Our house was an old Tudor mansion. My father was very particular in keeping the smallest peculiarities of his home unaltered. Thus, the many peaks and gables, the numerous turrets, and all of the windows with their quaint lozenge panes set in lead remained just as they had been three centuries back. Over and above the quaint melancholy of our dwelling, with the deep woods of its park and sullen waters of the sea, our neighborhood was small and primitive, and the people around us were ignorant and clung to their ancient ideas and traditions.

Thus, it was a superstitious atmosphere that we children were raised in, and we heard from our infancy countless tales of horror—some were doubtlessly just fables, others were legends of dark deeds of the olden times.

Our mother had died when we were young and our other parent being (though a kind father) obsessed with the affairs of the town, acting as both magistrate and landlord—there was no one to check the wave of dark and twisted tales our little minds were filled with by the nurses and servants.

As the years went on, however, the old ghostly tales lost their hold over us, and our undisciplined minds were turned more toward balls, dresses, and partners—airy and trivial matters more welcome to our riper age.

It was at a county assembly that Reginald and I first met—met and loved. Yes, I am sure that he loved me with all his heart. It was not as deep a heart as some, I have thought in my grief and anger, but I never doubted its truth and honesty.

Reginald's father and mine approved of our growing attachment. As for myself, I know I was so happy then—I look back upon those fleeting moments as on some delicious dream.

And now, the change. I have lingered on my childish memories, my bright and happy youth, and now I must tell you the rest—the blight and the sorrow.

It was Christmas, always a joyful and hospitable time in the country, especially in such an old hall as our home, where quaint customs and frolics were clung to as part of the very building itself.

The hall was full of guests—so full that there was a great difficulty in providing sleeping accommodations for everyone. Several narrow, dark chambers in the turrets—pigeon-holes as we called the rooms that had been good enough for the stately gentlemen of Elizabeth's reign—were now allotted to the bachelors, after having been empty for over a century. All the spare rooms in the body and wings of the hall were full, of course, and the servants who had been brought down were lodged at the farm and the nearby inn.

At last, the unexpected arrival of an elderly relative (who had been asked months before but was not expected) caused a great bit of commotion. My aunts went about wringing their hands. Lady Speldhurst was a person of some consequence—she was a distant cousin and had been on cool terms with all of us for years, on account of some imagined slight when she had paid her *last* visit at the time of my christening. She was seventy years old, infirm, rich, and testy. Moreover, she was my godmother, though I had forgotten that fact. But it seemed that although I had no expectations of a legacy in my favor, my aunts had done so for me. Aunt Margaret was especially eloquent on the subject.

"There isn't a room left!" she cried. "We cannot put Lady Speldhurst into the turrets. Yet where *is* she to sleep? And Rosa's godmother, too! Poor dear child! How dreadful! After all these years of estrangement, and with a hundred thousand pounds in funds and no comfortable, warm room at her disposal—and Christmas… of all times in the year!"

What *was* to be done? My aunts could not give up their own rooms to Lady Speldhurst because they had already given them up to some of the married guests.

My father was the most hospitable of men, but he suffered from arthritis and gout. His sisters-in-law didn't dare propose to move him from his quarters.

The matter ended in my giving up my room. I was reluctant to make the offer, which surprised myself. Was it a boding of evil to come? I cannot say. We are strangely and wonderfully made. It may have been.

At any rate, I do not think it was any selfish unwillingness to make an old and infirm lady comfortable by a simple sacrifice. I was perfectly healthy and strong. The weather was not cold for the time of year. It was a dark, moist Yule—not a snowy one, though snow brooded overhead in the dark clouds. I *did* make the offer with a laugh.

My sisters laughed too and made jokes about my wish to be kind to my godmother.

"She is a fairy godmother, Rosa," Minnie said, "and you know she was insulted at your christening and went away, muttering something about vengeance. Here she is coming back to see you. I hope she brings some gifts with her."

I thought little of Lady Speldhurst and her possible gifts. I didn't care much for the wonderful fortune my aunts whispered about so mysteriously. But since then, I have wondered if I had been selfish or obstinate and refused to give up my room for the expected kinswoman, would my life have been so altered? But then Lucy or Minnie would have offered instead and they would have been sacrificed... better that the blow fell where it did than on those dear ones.

The chamber I moved to was a little triangular room in the western wing and was only reached by marching past the picture gallery or by climbing a little flight of stone stairs that led directly upwards from a low arched doorway in the garden.

There was one more room on the same landing—merely a receptacle for broken furniture, shattered toys, and all the lumber that might accumulate in a country house.

The room I was to inhabit for a few nights was a tapestry-hung apartment, with faded green curtains, strangely enough with a new carpet, and the bright, fresh hangings of the bed, which had been put up quickly. The furniture was half old, half new, and on the dressing-table stood a very quaint oval mirror, in a frame of black wood—unpolished ebony, I think. I can remember the very pattern of the carpet, the number of chairs, the position of the bed, the figures on the tapestry. Not only can I recollect the color of the dress I wore on that fateful evening, but the arrangement of every scrap of lace and ribbon, of every flower, every jewel, with perfect memory.

My maid had barely finished spreading out my various articles of attire for the evening (when there was to be a great dinner party) when the rumble of a carriage announced that Lady Speldhurst had arrived.

The short winter's day drew to a close, and a large number of guests had gathered together in the ample drawing-room, around the blazing fire, after dinner.

I remember that my father was not with us at first. There were some squires of the hard-riding, hard-drinking type that still lingered over their port in the dining room, and the host, of course, could not leave them.

But the ladies and all the younger gentlemen—both those who slept under our roof and those who would have a dozen miles of fog to encounter on their way home—were all together.

Do I need to say that Reginald was there? He sat near me—my accepted lover, my future husband. We were to be married in the spring.

My sisters were not far off. They, too, had found eyes that sparkled and softened in meeting theirs, had found hearts that beat in time with their own.

The room, a large and lofty one with an arched roof, had somewhat of a somber feeling about it from being wainscoted and ceiled with polished black oak of a great age. There were mirrors, and there were pictures on the walls, and handsome furniture, and marble chimneypieces, and a beautiful carpet... but these merely appeared as bright spots on the dark background of the Elizabethan woodwork. Many lights were burning, but the blackness of the walls and roof seemed to swallow up their rays, like the mouth of a cavern. A hundred candles could not have given that room the cheerful lightness of a modern drawing-room.

But the gloomy richness of the panels matched well with the ruddy gleam from the enormous wood fire, in which crackling and glowing, now lay the mighty Yule log. Quite a blood-red luster poured forth from the fire and quivered on the walls of the ceiling.

We had gathered around the vast antique hearth in a wide circle. The quivering light of the fire and candles fell upon us all, but not equally, for some were in shadow.

I still remember how tall and handsome Reginald looked that night—taller than anyone else there and full of high spirits. I, too, was in the highest spirits—never had my heart felt lighter. What a happy, joyful group we seemed—all except one.

Lady Speldhurst, dressed in gray silk and wearing a quaint headdress, sat in her armchair, facing the fire, very silent, with her hands and her sharp chin propped on a sort of ivory-handled crutch that she walked with (for she was lame), peering at me with half-shut eyes. She was a little old woman with very keen and delicate French features. Her gray silk dress, her spotless lace, old-fashioned jewels, and overall neatness were well suited to the intelligence of her face, with its thin lips and black piercing eyes, undimmed by age. Those eyes made me uncomfortable, despite my laughter, as they followed my every movement with curious scrutiny.

Still, I was very merry. Even my sisters wondered why I was laughing so much.

I have heard since then of the Scottish belief that those doomed to some great calamity become *fey* and are overcome with laughter and merriment just before the blow falls. If ever a mortal was *fey*, then I was so on that evening.

Still, though, I fought to ignore the feeling of Lady Speldhurst's eyes upon me. Others noticed her scrutiny of me too but wrote it off as an eccentricity of a person always reputed whimsical, to say the least.

This disagreeable sensation lasted only a few moments. After a short pause, my aunt took over the conversation, and we found ourselves listening to a weird legend which the old lady told exceedingly well.

One tale led to another. Everyone was called on in turn to contribute to the public entertainment, and story after story, always relating to demonology or witchcraft, succeeded in scaring us.

It was Christmas—the season for such tales—and the old room, with its dusky walls and pictures and vaulted ceiling drinking up the light so greedily, seemed like the perfect place for such lore.

The huge logs crackled and burned with glowing warmth. The blood-red glare of the Yule log flashed on the faces of the listeners and narrator, on the portraits, and the holly wreathed about their frames, and the upright old dame in her antiquated dress and trinkets, like one of the original pictures stepped from the canvas to join the circle. It threw a shimmering luster of an ominously ruddy hue upon the oaken panels. No wonder that the ghost and goblin stories had a new zest! No wonder that the blood of the more timid chilled and curdled, that their flesh crept, and their hearts beat fast, and the girls peeped fearfully over their shoulders, and huddled close together like frightened sheep, and half-fancied they saw some impish and malignant face smiling at them from the darkest corners of the old room.

Gradually, my high spirits died out, and I felt the childish fears—long-latent, long-forgotten—washing over me. I followed each story with painful interest—I did not stop to ask myself if I believed in any of them. I listened, and my fear grew—the blind, irrational fear of our nursery days. I am sure most of the other ladies present, young or middle-aged, were also affected by these old traditional tales. But with them, the impression these stories had would die out by the morning, when the bright sun would shine on the frosted boughs.

Before we had finished these ghostly tales, my father and the other squires came in. We quickly stopped, ashamed to speak of such matters before these newcomers—hard-headed, unimaginative men who had no sympathy for legends. There was now a stir and bustle.

Servants were passing out tea and coffee, and other refreshments. Then there was a little music and singing. I sang a duet with Reginald, who had a fine voice and good musical skill. I remember that everyone praised my singing, and I, myself, was surprised at the power of my own voice, doubtless due to my excited nerves and mind.

Then I heard someone say to another that I was by far the cleverest of the squire's daughters, as well as the prettiest. It did not make me proud or vain. I had no rivalry with Lucy and Minnie. But Reginald whispered some fond words softly in my ear a little before he mounted his horse to set off homewards, which *did* make me happy and proud. And to think that the next time we met... but I forgave him long ago.

Now the shawls and cloaks were requested, carriages rolled up to the porch, and the guests gradually departed. At last, no one was left but those visitors staying in the house.

Then my father, who had been called out to speak with the bailiff of the estate, came back, clearly annoyed.

"I've just been told a very strange story," he began. "My bailiff just informed me that we lost four of the finest ewes from that little flock in the south. The poor creatures were destroyed in so strange a manner, their carcasses are horribly mangled."

Most of us uttered some expression of pity or surprise, and some suggested that a vicious dog was probably the culprit.

"It would seem so," my father said. "It clearly seems the work of a dog. Yet all the men agree that no dog as vicious as that exists near us. Dogs are scarce except the shepherds' collies and the sporting dogs secured in the yards. Yet the sheep are gnawed and bitten—you can see the teeth marks. Something has done this and has torn their bodies apart like a wolf, but apparently, it was only to suck the blood, for little or no flesh is gone."

"How strange!" several voices cried.

Then some of the gentlemen remembered rumors of dogs so addicted to killing sheep that they destroyed entire flocks.

My father shook his head. "I have heard of such cases too," he said. "But in this instance, I am tempted to think the malice of some unknown enemy is at work. The teeth of a dog have been busy, no doubt, but the poor sheep have been mutilated in a fantastic manner, as strange as it is horrible. Their hearts, in particular, have been torn out and found several paces away, half-gnawed. Also, the men insist that they found a human footprint in the soft mud. And near it—this."

He held up what seemed to be a broken link of a rusted iron chain. There were cries of wonder and alarm and many shrewd conjectures, but none seemed exactly to suit the details of the case.

When my father went on to say that two lambs of the same valuable breed had perished in the same peculiar manner three days ago (also found mangled and stained), the amazement reached a higher pitch.

Old Lady Speldhurst listened with calm, intelligent attention but didn't say a word. At length, she said to my father, "Try to remember—have you any enemies among your neighbors?"

My father furrowed his brow. "None that I know of," he replied. Indeed, he was a popular man and a kind landlord.

"Lucky for you," said the old dame, with one of her grim smiles.

It was now late, and we retired to rest. One by one, the guests dropped off. I was the member of the family selected to escort old Lady Speldhurst to her room—the room I had vacated for her.

I felt a great dislike for my godmother, but my aunts insisted that I try to reacquaint myself with someone who had so much to leave that I could do nothing but comply.

The old woman hobbled up the broad oaken stairs, propped on my arm and her ivory crutch.

The room had never looked more welcoming and pretty, with its brisk fire, modern furniture, and the fancy French paper on the walls.

"A nice room, my dear. And I ought to thank you for it since my maid tells me it is yours," her ladyship said. "But I am pretty sure you regret your generosity to me after all those ghost stories. No doubt you tremble to think of a strange bed and chamber."

I made some commonplace reply.

The old lady arched her eyebrows. "Where have they put you, child?" she asked. "In some loft in the turrets? Or in a lumber-room—a regular ghost trap? I can hear your heart beating with fear at this very moment. You are not fit to be alone."

I tried to call up my pride and laugh off the accusation against my courage, all the more, perhaps, because I felt it was true. "Is there anything I can get you, Lady Speldhurst?" I asked, trying to feign a yawn of sleepiness.

The old dame's keen eyes were upon me. "I rather like you, my dear," she said, "and I liked your mother well enough before she treated me so shamefully about the christening dinner. Now, I know you are frightened and fearful, and if an owl should simply flap outside your window tonight, it might drive you into fits. There is a nice sofa-bed in this dressing closet—call your maid to arrange it for you, and you can sleep there snugly, under the old witch's protection. No goblin would dare hurt you, and no one will be a bit the wiser or question if you were afraid."

How little I knew what hung in the balance of my refusal or acceptance of that trivial offer! Had the veil of the future been lifted for one instant! But that veil was impenetrable to our gaze. Yet perhaps *she* had a glimpse of the dim vista beyond... she who made the offer. For when I declined with a laugh, she said in a thoughtful manner, "Well, well! We must all make our own way through life. Goodnight, child… pleasant dreams!"

And with that, I softly closed the door. As I did so, she looked around at me with a glance I have never forgotten—half-malicious, half-sad—as if she had seen the doom that was to devour my young hopes. It may have been mere eccentricity, the odd fantasy of a crooked mind, the whimsical conduct of a cynical person, triumphant in the power of frightening youth and beauty. Or, I have since thought, it may have been that this one guest possessed such a gift as the Highland "second-sight"—a sad gift that is useless to the possessor but still enough to convey a dim sense of coming evil and impending doom. And yet, had she really known what was in store for me—what lurked behind the veil of the future—not even her dry heart could have remained passive toward me. She would have snatched me back. But, sadly, she had no such power.

I left her door. As I crossed the landing, a bright gleam came from another room, whose door was left ajar. It (the light) fell like a bar of golden sheen across my path.

As I approached, the door opened, and my sister, Lucy, who had been watching for me came out. She was already in a white cashmere wrapper, over which her loosened hair hung darkly and heavily, like tangles of silk.

"Rosa, love," she whispered, "Minnie and I can't bear the idea of you sleeping out there, all alone, in that solitary room—the very room that Nurse Sherrard used to talk about! So, as you know, Minnie has given up her room and has come to sleep in mine. Still, we so wish that you would sleep with us tonight. I could make up a bed on the sofa for myself, or you—and—"

I stopped Lucy's mouth with a kiss. I declined her offer. I would not listen to it. In fact, my pride was up in arms, and I felt I would rather pass the night in the churchyard itself than accept a proposal dictated by the notion that my nerves were shaken by the ghostly lore we had been sharing, that I was a weak superstitious creature, unable to pass a night in a strange chamber. So, I would not listen to Lucy, but kissed her, bade her goodnight, and went on my way laughing to show my light heart.

Yet, as I looked back in the dark corridor and saw the friendly door still ajar, the yellow bar of light still crossing from wall to wall, the sweet, kind face still peering after me from amid its clustering curls, I felt a thrill of sympathy—a wish to return, a yearning for human love and companionship.

False shame was strongest and conquered.

I waved a cheerful adieu.

I turned the corner, and peeping over my shoulder, I saw the door close—the bar of yellow light was no longer there in the dark passage. I thought, at that instant, that I heard a heavy sigh. I looked around sharply, but no one was there. No door was open, yet I fancied (and fancied with wonderful vividness) that I did hear an actual sigh breathed not far off and plainly distinguishable from the groan of the sycamore branches as the wind tossed them to and fro in the darkness. If ever a mortal's good angel had cause to sigh for sorrow (not sin), mine had cause to mourn that night.

I had to go through the picture gallery. I had never entered this apartment by candlelight before, and I was struck by the gloomy array of the tall portraits, gazing moodily from the canvas onto the window panes which rattled to the blast of wind that swept howling by. Many of the faces looked stern and very different from their daylight expression. In others, a tiny flickering smile seemed to mock me as my candle illuminated them. And in all of them, the eyes (as usual with artistic portraits) seemed to follow my motions with a scrutiny and an interest. I felt ill at ease under this stony gaze, though conscious of how absurd my fears were. I called upon a smile as if acting a part under the eyes of fellow human beings rather than their mere shadows on the wall. I even laughed as I confronted them.

My short-lived laugh didn't even have the chance to echo among the hollow armor and arched ceiling before I continued on my way in silence.

I have spoken of the armor. Indeed, there was a fine collection of plate and mail, for my father was an enthusiastic collector. In particular, there were two suits of black armor, erect and topped with helmets with closed visors, which stood as if two mailed champions were guarding the gallery and its treasures. I had often seen these, of course, but never by night, and never when my thoughts were filled with ghosts and goblins.

As I approached the Black Knights, as we had dubbed them, a wild notion seized on me that the figures moved, that men were concealed in the hollow shells which had once been worn in tournaments and battles. I knew the idea was childish, yet I was on edge and believed I could see eyes glaring at me from the eyelet holes in the visors.

I passed them, and then my imagination told me that the figures followed me with stealthy strides. I heard a clatter of steel, caused, I am sure, by a violent gust of wind sweeping the gallery through the crevices of the old windows. With a stifled shriek, I rushed to the door, opened it, darted inside, and clapped it shut with a bang that echoed through the whole wing of the house.

It was then, by a sudden and uncommon revulsion of feeling, that I shook off my aimless terrors, blushed at my weakness, and was suddenly relieved that I was the only one in the room, so I was the only witness to my tremors.

As I entered my chamber, I thought I heard something stir in the neglected lumber-room, which was the only neighboring apartment. But I was determined to have no more panics and resolutely shut my ears to this slight, transient noise, which had nothing unnatural about it—for surely between bats and wind, an old manor-house on a stormy night needs no sprites to disturb it.

So, I entered my room and rang for my maid. As I did so, I looked around me, and a most unexplainable disgust for my temporary abode came over me in spite of my best efforts. It was no more to be shaken off than a chill is to be shaken off when we enter some damp cave. And, rely upon it, the feeling of dislike and apprehension with which we regard at first sight certain people and places was not implanted in us without some wholesome purpose. I admit it is irrational—mere animal instinct—but is not instinct God's gift, and is it for us to despise it? It is by instinct that children know their friends from their enemies—that they distinguish with such certainty between those who like them and those who only flatter and hate them. Dogs do the same—they will fawn on one person, and they slink snarling from another. Show me a man whom children and dogs shrink from, and I will show you a false, bad man—lies on his lips and murder in his heart. No... let none despise the heaven-sent gift of innate intuition.

I felt this intuition so strongly as I looked around me in my new sleeping room, and yet I could find no logical reason for my dislike.

It was a very good room, after all, now that the green curtains were drawn, the fire burning bright and clear, candles burning on the mantle, and the various familiar toiletries arranged as usual. The bed, too, looked peaceful and inviting—a pretty little white bed, not at all the large funeral sort of couch which haunted chambers usually contained.

My maid entered and assisted me in laying aside the dress and ornaments I had worn and arranged my hair, as usual, prattling all the while. I rarely cared to converse with servants, but on that night, a sort of dread of being left alone—a longing to keep some human being near me—possessed me, and I encouraged the girl to gossip so that her duties took her half an hour longer than usual. At last, however, she had done all that could be done, and all my questions were answered, and my orders for the next day were given, and the clock on the turret struck one.

Then Mary, yawning, left the room.

The shutting of the door, gently as it was, affected me rather unpleasantly. I took a dislike to the curtains, the tapestry, the dingey pictures—everything. I hated the room once again. I fought the urge to put on a cloak, run, half-dressed, to my sisters' chamber, and say I had changed my mind and had come for shelter.

But they must be asleep, I thought. *I couldn't be so rude as to wake them.*

I said my prayers with unusual earnestness and a heavy heart. I extinguished the candles and was just about to lay my head on my pillow when the idea seized me that I should lock the door.

The candles were extinguished, but the firelight was enough to guide me. I scurried to the door. There was a lock, but it was rusty, and my utmost strength could not turn the key. The bolt was broken and worthless. Trying to comfort myself, I remembered that I had never needed a lock before and returned to my bed.

I lay awake for a good while, watching the red glow of the burning coals in the grate. I was quiet now and more composed. Even the light gossip of the maid, full of petty human cares and joys, had done me good—diverted my thoughts from brooding.

I was at the point of dropping into sleep when I was twice disturbed. Once, by an owl, hooting in the ivy outside—not an unusual sound, but harsh and melancholy—and again by a long and mournful howling by the mastiff, chained in the yard beyond the wing. It was a long-drawn howling—such a note as the vulgar declare to herald a death in the family.

This was a thought that I have never shared. Yet I could not help feeling that the dog's mournful moans were sad and terrified, not at all like his fierce, honest bark of anger. Rather, it was as if something evil was afoot.

Soon I fell asleep.

How long I slept, I never knew. I awoke at once, with that abrupt start which we all know well and which carries us in a second from utter unconsciousness to the full use of our faculties.

The fire was still burning but was very low, and half of the room was in deep shadow. I knew, I felt, that some person or thing was in the room, although I could see nothing unusual in the feeble light. Yet, it was a sense of danger that had aroused me from my slumber. I experienced, while still asleep, the chill and shock of sudden alarm, and I knew, even in the act of throwing off sleep like a mantle, *why* I awoke and that some intruder was present. Yet though I listened intently, I could hear no sound except the faint murmur of the fire—the dropping of cinder from the bars—and the loud, irregular beatings of my own heart.

Beyond this silence, by some intuition, I knew that I had not been deceived by a dream and felt certain that I was not alone. I waited. My heart beat on, quicker and more sudden in its pulsations, as a bird in a cage might flutter in the presence of a hawk.

And then I heard a faint but quite distinct sound—the clank of iron, the rattling of a chain!

I ventured to lift my head from the pillow.

Dim and uncertain as the light was, I saw the curtains of my bed shake and caught a glimpse of something beyond, a darker spot in the darkness.

This confirmation of my fears did not surprise me so much as it shocked me. I tried to cry out loud but could not utter a word.

The chain rattled again, and this time, the noise was louder and clearer. But though I strained my eyes, they could not penetrate the obscurity that shrouded the other end of the chamber, from whence the sullen clanking came.

In a moment, several distinct trains of thought, like many-colored strands of thread twining into one, became palpable to my mind's eye. Was it a robber? Could it be a supernatural visitor? Or was I the victim of a cruel trick, such as I had heard of, and which some thoughtless persons love to practice on the timid, reckless of its dangerous results?

And then a new idea, with some ray of comfort in it, suggested itself. There was a fine young dog of the Newfoundland breed, a favorite of my father's, which was usually chained by night in an outhouse. Neptune might have broken loose, found his way to my room, and, finding the door not quite closed, have pushed it open and entered.

I breathed more freely as this harmless interpretation of the noise forced itself upon me. It was—it must be—the dog, and I was distressing myself uselessly. I resolved to call to him—I tried to call his name—but a secret apprehension stopped me, and I was mute. Then the chain clanked nearer and nearer to the bed, and I saw a dusky shapeless mass appear between the curtains on the opposite side to where I was laying.

How I longed to hear the whine of the poor animal that I hoped might be the cause of my alarm. But no. I heard no sound save the rustle of the curtains and the clash of the iron chain.

Just then, the dying flame of the fire leaped up, and with one sweeping hurried glance, I saw that the door was shut and—horror!—it was not a dog!

It had the semblance of a human form that threw itself heavily on the bed, outside the clothes, and laid there, huge and dark, in the red gleam that treacherously died away after showing so much to frighten and sunk into dull darkness.

There was now no light left, though the red cinders still glowed with a ruddy gleam, like the eyes of wild beasts. The chain rattled no more.

I tried to speak, to scream wildly for help—my mouth was parched, my tongue refused to obey. I could not utter a cry, and indeed, who could have heard me, alone as I was in that solitary chamber, with no living neighbor, and the picture-gallery between me and any aid that even the loudest, most piercing shriek could summon. And the storm that howled outside would have drowned my voice, even if help had been at hand.

To call aloud—to demand who was there—alas! How useless! How perilous! If the intruder were a robber, my outcries would make him furious. As for a trick... that seemed impossible. And yet, *what* lay by my side, now wholly unseen?

I tried to pray out loud, as there rushed to my memory a flood of weird legends—the dreaded yet fascinating lore of my childhood. I had heard and read of the spirits of wicked men forced to revisit the scenes of their earthly crimes—of demons that lurked in certain cursed spots—of the ghoul and vampire of the East, sneaking among the graves that rifled for their ghostly banquets, and I shuddered as I gazed on the blank darkness where I knew it lay.

It stirred—moaned hoarsely—and again I heard the chain clank close beside me... so close that it must have almost touched me. I pulled away from it, shrinking away in loathing and terror of the evil thing. I wasn't sure what it was, but I felt that something malignant was near.

In the extremity of my fear, I dared not speak. I was desperate to be quiet even as I backed away. I had some wild hope that it—the phantom, the creature, whatever it was—had not discovered my presence in the room.

And then I remembered all of the events of the night—Lady Speldhurst's ill-omened predictions, her half-warnings, her strange look as we parted, my sister's persuasions, my terror in the gallery, the remark that "this was the room Nurse Sherrard used to talk of." And then memory stimulated by fear, recalled the long-forgotten past, the ill-repute of this disused chamber, the sins it had witnessed, the blood spilled, the poison administered by such hate within its walls, and tradition which called it haunted.

The green room—I remembered now how fearfully the servants avoided it—how it was rarely mentioned, and in whispers, when we were children, and how we had regarded it as a mysterious region, unfit for mortal habitation.

Was It—the dark form with the chain—a creature of this world or a specter? And again—more dreadful still—could it be that the corpses of the wicked men were forced to rise and haunt the places where they had wrought their evil deeds in life? Could this be my grisly neighbor?

The chain rattled faintly. My hair bristled. My eyeballs seemed to pop from their sockets. There was sweat upon my brow. My heart struggled to beat as if I were crushed beneath some great weight. Sometimes it appeared to stop its frenzied beatings, sometimes its pulsations were fierce and hurried. My breath came short and with extreme difficulty. I shivered as if I was cold, yet I feared to stir.

It moved, it moaned, its fetters clanked dismally, the couch creaked and shook. This was no phantom—no airy specter. But its very solidity, its palpable presence, were a thousand times more terrible.

I felt that I was in the very grasp of what could not only terrify but harm—of something whose contact sickened the soul with deathly fear.

I made a desperate decision: I glided from the bed, seized a blanket, threw it around me, and tried to grope my way to the door.

My heart beat high at the hope of escape. But I had scarcely taken one step before the moaning began again, it transformed into a threatening growl that would have suited a wolf's throat and a hand clutched at my sleeve. I stood motionless. The muttering growl sank to a moan again. The chain sounded no more, but still, the hand held its grip on my garment, and I feared to move.

It knew of my presence, then.

My mind reeled, the blood boiled in my ears, and my knees lost all strength while my heart panted like that of a deer in the wolf's jaws.

I sank back, and the numbing power of terror reduced me to a state of stupor.

When my full consciousness returned, I was sitting on the edge of the bed, shivering with cold and bare-footed. All was silent, but I felt that my unearthly visitor still clutched my sleeve.

The silence lasted a long time. Then a chuckling laugh followed, that froze my very marrow, and then a wailing moan, and this was succeeded by silence.

Hours may have passed—now... although the tumult of my own heart prevented me from hearing the clock strike, hours *must* have passed—but the hours seemed like ages. And how were they spent? Hideous visions passed before my aching eyes that I dared not close but which gazed ever into the darkness where it lay—my dreaded companion.

I pictured it in every horrible form which an excited imagination could summon up: now as a skeleton, with hollow eyes-holes and grinning fleshless jaws; now as a vampire with a pale face and slender form, the wet mouth dripping with blood.

Would it ever be light?!

And yet, when the day should dawn, I should be forced to see it face to face. I had heard the specter and fiend are compelled to fade as morning brightened, but this creature was too real, too foul a thing of earth, to vanish as the cock crowed.

The cold prevailed, and my teeth chattered, and I shivered from head to toe, and yet there was an agonizing sweat still bursting on my brow.

Some instinct made me snatch at a shawl that lay on a chair within reach and wrap it around me.

The moaning began once again and the chain stirred. Then I sank into apathy, like a criminal facing the gallows between their rounds of torture. Hours flew by, and I remained like a statue of ice, rigid and mute.

Shuddering but urged by the impulse that rivets the gaze of the bird upon the snake, I turned to see the horror of the night.

Yes, it was no fevered dream, no hallucination of sickness, no airy phantom unable to face the dawn. In the sickly light, I saw it lying on the bed with its grim head on the pillow. A man? Or a corpse arisen from its unhallowed grave and awaiting the demon that animated it?

There it lay—a gaunt, gigantic form, wasted to a skeleton, half-clad, foul with dust and clotted gore, its huge limbs flung upon the couch as if at random, its shaggy hair streaming over the pillows like a lion's mane. Its face was toward me. Oh, the wild hideousness of that face, even in sleep! In features, it was human, even through its horrid mask of mud and half-dried bloody cuts, but the expression was brutish and savagely fierce. The white teeth were visible between the parted lips, in a malignant grin, and the tangled hair and beard were mixed in leonine confusion, and there were scars disfiguring the brow. Round the creature's waist was a ring of iron, to which was attached a heavy but broken chain—the chain I had heard clanking.

With a second glance, I noted that part of the chain was wrapped in straw to prevent its galling the wearer. The creature—I cannot call it a man—had the marks of fetters on its wrists, the bony arm that protruded through one tattered sleeve was scarred and bruised, the feet were bare and lacerated by pebbles, and one of them was wounded and wrapped in a morsel of a rag. And the lean hands, one of which held my sleeve, were armed with talons like an eagle's.

In an instant, the horrid truth flashed upon me—I was in the grasp of a madman. Better the phantom that scares the sight than the wild beast that tears the quivering flesh—the pitiless human brute that has no heart to be softened, no reason at whose bar to plead, no compassion, nothing of a man except the form and the cunning.

I gasped in terror. Ah! The mystery of those boney fingers, those gory wolfish jaws! That face... all stained with dried black blood.

The slain sheep, so mangled with such fantastic butchery—the print of the naked foot—all were explained. And the chain, the broken link of which was found near the slaughtered animals—it came from his broken chain—the chain he had snapped, doubtless, in his escape from the asylum where his raging frenzy had been fettered and bound. In vain! In vain! How did this grisly Samson break his manacles and prison bars—how had he eluded guardian and keep and a hostile world, and come hither on his wild way, hunted like a beast of prey, and snatching his hideous banquet like a beast of prey, too?

Yet, through the tatters of his mean and ragged garb, I could see the scars of violence, cruel and foolish, with which men at that time tried to tame the might of madness. The scourge—its marks were there—and the scars of the hard iron cuffs, and many a welt and cut, that told a dismal tale of abuse.

But now he was loose, free to play the brute—the baited, tortured brute that they had made him—now without the cage and ready to gloat over the victims his strength could overpower. Horror! Horror! I was the prey—the victim—already in the tiger's clutch. A deadly sickness came over me, and the iron entered into my soul, and I longed to scream and was dumb!

I died a thousand deaths as that awful morning wore on. I dared not faint. But words cannot paint how I suffered as I waited—waited till the moment when he should open his eyes and be aware of my presence, for I was assured he did not know of it yet.

He had entered the chamber as a lair, weary and gorged with his horrid ordeal, and he had flung himself down to sleep without a suspicion that he was not alone. Even his grasping my sleeve was doubtless an act done betwixt sleeping and waking, like his unconscious moans and laughter, in some frightful dream.

Hours went on. Then I trembled as I thought that soon the house would stir, that my maid would come to call me as usual and wake that ghastly sleeper. And wouldn't he have time to rip me apart just as he tore apart the sheep before any help could arrive?

At last, what I had dreaded had come to pass—a light footstep on the landing and a tap at the door. A pause and then the tapping renewed and this time more loudly.

The madman stretched his limbs and uttered his moaning cry, and his eyes slowly opened—very slowly—and met mine.

The maid waited a while before she knocked for the third time.

I trembled, lest she should open the door uninvited—see that grim thing and by her screams and terror bring about the worst. Long before strong men could arrive, I knew that I would be dead—and what a death!

The maid waited, no doubt surprised at my unusually sound slumber—for I was generally a light sleeper and an early riser—but reluctant to deviate from habit by entering without permission.

I was still alone with the thing in man's shape, but he was awake now. I saw the wondering surprise in his haggard bloodshot eyes. I saw him stare at me half vacantly, then with a crafty yet wondering look. And then I saw the devil of murder begin to peep forth from those hideous eyes, and the lips parted in a sneer, and the wolfish teeth were bared.

But I was not what I had been. Fear gave me a new and a desperate composure—a courage foreign to my nature. I had heard of the best method of managing the insane. I could at least try... I *did* try.

Calmly, wondering at my own feigned calm, I held the glare of those terrible eyes. Steady and undaunted was my gaze—motionless. I marveled at myself, but in that agony of sickening terror, I was *outwardly* firm.

They sank, abashed, those dreadful eyes before the gaze of a helpless girl. And the shame that is never absent from insanity bears down the pride of strength, the bloody cravings of the wild beast.

The lunatic moaned and drooped his shaggy head between his gaunt squalid hands.

I didn't waste a moment.

I rose and with one spring, reached the door, tore it open, and with a shriek, rushed through, caught the wondering girl by the arm, and crying to her to run for her life, rushed like the wind along the gallery, down the corridor, down the stairs.

Mary's screams filled the house as she fled beside me. I heard a long-drawn, raging cry, the roar of a wild animal mocked by its prey, and I knew that It was behind me.

I never turned my head—I flew rather than ran.

I was in the hall already. There was a rush of many feet, an outcry of many voices, a sound of scuffling feet, and brutal yells, and oaths, and heavy blows, and I fell to the ground, crying, "Save me!" and fainted.

I awoke from a delirious trance. Kind faces were around my bed, loving looks were cast my way by one and all, by my dear father and dear sisters, but I scarcely saw them before I fainted again…

When I recovered from that long illness, through which I had been nursed so tenderly, the pitying looks I met made me tremble. I asked for a looking-glass. It was long denied to me, but at last, a mirror was brought.

My youth was gone in one fell swoop. The glass showed me a livid and haggard face, blanched and bloodless as one who sees a specter. In the ashen lips, wrinkled brow, and dim eyes, I could trace nothing of my old self. The hair, too, thick and rich before was now as white as snow, and in one night, the ravages of half a century had passed over my face. Nor have my nerves ever recovered their tone after that dire shock.

Can you wonder that my life was ruined and that my lover shrank away from me?

I am old now—old and alone.

My sisters would have had me live with them, but I chose not to sadden their genial homes with my phantom face and dead eyes.

Reginald married another. He has been dead for many years now. I never ceased to love him, though he left me when I needed him most of all.

The sad weird is nearly over now. I am old, and near the end, and happy for it. I have not been bitter or hard, but I cannot bear to see many people and am happiest alone. I try to do what good I can with the worthless wealth Lady Speldhurst left me, for, at my wish, my portion was shared between my sisters. What need do I have for an inheritance? I, the shattered woman, made by that one night of horror!

Was It an Illusion?
A Parson's Story
By: Amelia B. Edwards
1881

The story that I am about to tell you happened to myself some sixteen or eighteen years ago. At the time, I served Her Majesty as an Inspector of Schools. Now, an inspector is always on the move, and I was still young enough to enjoy a life of constant travel.

Of course, there are worse ways an unbeneficed parson could spend their days. In remote villages where visitors are scarce, his annual visit is an important event—at the end of a long day's work, when he would rather return to his quiet country inn, he generally finds himself the guest at someone's table.

My first assignment was to a West of England district inhabited mostly by my friends and acquaintances. You can imagine my annoyance when I was transferred to what a policeman would call "a new beat" up in the North. Unfortunately, my new region was thinly populated but three times larger than my old one, making it nearly unmanageable. It was surrounded by barren hills and cut off from the main railway lines. Somehow, it had about every inconvenience that a district could possess. The villages were wide apart, usually separated by moors, and instead of being able to hop into a warm railway compartment, I now had to spend my time in cold hired vehicles.

I had been in this district for about three months, and winter was at hand when I paid my first visit to Pit End, a small hamlet in the northernmost corner of my county, twenty-two miles from the nearest station. Having stayed overnight in a place called Drumley and inspected Drumley schools in the morning, I started for Pit End, with fourteen miles of railway and twenty-two of hilly roads between myself and my destination. I tried to inquire about Pit End before leaving Drumley, but neither the schoolmaster nor the landlord of the inn knew much more about Pit End than its name. It would seem my predecessor arrived in Pit End from the opposite direction—the roads, though longer, were less hilly that way. They assured me that the town had an inn of some kind, but they knew nothing more than that.

With what little information I could gather, I set out for Pit End. My fourteen miles on the railway soon ended at a place called Bramsford Road. From there, I took an omnibus to a dull little town called Bramsford Market. Here I found a horse and cart to carry me to my destination—the horse being a skinny gray mare that looked more like a camel. From Bramsford Market, the way lay over a series of long hills, rising to a barren plateau. It was a dark, cold afternoon in mid-November, growing darker and colder as the day waned and the east wind picked up.

"How much further, driver?" I asked as we began to climb the steepest hill we'd met thus far.

He turned a straw in his mouth and grunted something about "fewr 'r foive mile by the road."

And then I learned that by turning off the road at a point and taking a footpath across the fields, I might get to Pit End faster. I decided, therefore, to walk the rest of the way. Setting off at a good pace toward the top of the hill, I soon lost sight of my driver and his horse. I found the footpath without any difficulty next to the ruins of an old toll house.

The footpath led me across a barren slope divided by stone fences, with the occasional abandoned shed, tall chimney, or cinder mound, marking the site of a deserted mine. Meanwhile, a light fog was creeping up from the east, and dusk was fast approaching.

Now to lose your way in such a place at such an hour in the day would be bad enough, and the footpath—a poorly marked track—would be impossible to see in another ten minutes. I looked ahead anxiously, searching for some sign of civilization, and picked up my pace. I presently came to a point where the path divided: one way continued along an enclosure surrounded by barren trees, and the other struck off across an open meadow.

Which should I take?

By following the stone fence, I was sure to arrive at a lodge where I could get directions to Pit End. But I had no idea how large the park with its dark trees might be and how long it would take me before I arrived at the nearest lodge. But the meadow path might lead away from Pit End and take me in the opposite direction. There was no time to hesitate, so I chose the meadow.

Up until this moment, I had not met a living soul of whom to ask my way. It was, therefore, no surprise of my relief when I spotted a man emerging from the fog and moving toward me along the path. As we neared each other—I was marching quickly, he a bit more slowly—I noticed that he dragged his left foot, limping as he walked. It was, however, so dark and misty that it wasn't until we were within half a dozen yards of each other that I saw that he wore a dark suit and an Anglican felt hat and looked something like a minister. As soon as we were within speaking distance, I addressed him.

"Can you tell me if I am on the right path for Pit End? How far do I have to go?"

He continued walking, looking straight ahead and not hearing my question.

"I beg your pardon," I said, raising my voice, "but will this path take me to Pit End? And if so—"

He continued on without looking at me.

I stopped with the words on my lips. I turned to follow after him, but instead of following him, I stood in the middle of the path, confused.

Where did he go? And who was the young boy running up the path by which I had just come with a fishing rod over his shoulder? I could have sworn I didn't meet him or pass him. Where had he come from? And where was the man whom I had just spoken to not three seconds ago? Surely, with his limp, he could not have made it more than a few yards. I was so dumbfounded, I stood perfectly still, watching the boy disappear in the gloom under the trees.

Was I dreaming?

Meanwhile, darkness had arrived. Whether I was dreaming or not, I needed to continue on my journey. Turning my back on the last gleam of daylight, I stepped deeper into the fog. However, I was closer to my journey's end than I realized. The path ended at a turnstile which opened upon a lane, and at the bottom of the lane was the welcome glare of a blacksmith's forge.

Here, then, was Pit End. I found my cart with my luggage parked next to the door of the village inn, the gray mare was already in her stable for the night, and the landlord was waiting for my arrival.

The Greyhound (as the inn was called) was a modest place that I shared with a couple of farmers and a young man. Here I dined, wrote letters, chatted with the landlord for a bit, and learned a bit of the local news.

It seemed there was no resident parson at Pit End. The man who fulfilled the role now had three jobs in town, and

Pit End—being the smallest and most remote village—was only granted one church service a week on Sundays. The squire was an absent man, spending most of his time in Paris... but he happened to be home just now.

"He's been gone for five years and will be leaving again next week," the landlord explained. "It might be another five years before we see him at Blackwater Chase again."

Blackwater Chase. The name was not new to me, but I couldn't remember where I had heard it before.

"Even though he's rarely here, Mr. Wolstenholme is a pleasant gentleman and a good landlord," the man continued. "After all, Blackwater Chase is a lonesome sort of place for a young man to be."

It was at that moment that I remembered Phil Wolstenholme of Balliol. Once upon a time, he had invited me to come hunting at Blackwater Chase. That was twelve years ago when I was at school at Wadham. While I was studying and reading, Wolstenholme was boating, gambling, writing poetry, and hosting parties. He was at the center of a clique to which I did not belong.

Oh yes, I remembered him—his handsome face, luxurious rooms, his expensive taste, and his blind faith in his admirers. He graduated and left school with the reputation of having almost been expelled. How vividly it all came back to me—the old college life, the college friendships, the happy times that would never come again. It was only twelve years ago but somehow felt like half a century. And yet, after twelve long years, here we were—Wolstenholme and I—as neighbors just like our Oxford days! I wondered if he had changed much over the years… and if so, was it for the better?

Had his generosity developed into shining virtues, or had his follies hardened into vices?

Should I let him know I was in town and judge for myself? It was easy enough to send him a note in the morning. But was it worth it to rekindle an old friendship just to appease my curiosity? I thought long and hard on the matter as I sat next to my fire late into the night, and by the time I went to bed, I had nearly forgotten my encounter with the man who had vanished so mysteriously and the boy who seemed to come from nowhere.

The next morning, I had plenty of time to myself, so I wrote a quick note on my card and sent it up to the manor.

The day was just fine. I inspected the national schools from nine till about eleven. The wind had shifted to the north, the sun shone bright in the cold, and the grimy hamlet looked as bright as it could. The village was built along the side of a hill—the church and schools were along the top, and The Greyhound was at the bottom. I climbed the one rambling street, followed a path that skirted the churchyard, and found myself at the schools. These, along with the teachers' homes, formed three sides of a square, the fourth side consisting of an iron fence and gate. A sign over the main entrance recorded how *"These schoolhouses were rebuilt by Philip Wolstenholme, Esquire: AD 18—."*

"Mr. Wolstenholme is the Lord of the Manor," a soft voice whispered in my ear.

I turned and found a short, stout man standing behind me with a bundle of books under his arm.

"Are you the schoolmaster?" I asked, unable to remember his name and slightly puzzled as I felt I had seen his face before.

"Indeed I am. I assume I'm addressing Mr. Frazer?"

He had an unnerving face—pasty white and anxious. Even his eyes had a perpetual startled look to them, and I immediately felt uncomfortable.

"Yes," I replied, still wondering where I had seen him before. "My name is Frazer. Yours I believe is... is..." I reached into my pocket for my examination papers.

"Skelton." He saved me the trouble. Though I couldn't help but feel as if he had no desire to tell me his name—as if it were insignificant. "Ebenezer Skelton. Would you like to start with the boys?"

"That will be just fine."

As we moved to enter the schoolhouse, I noticed that the schoolmaster was lame. At that moment, I remembered where I had seen him before—he was the man I had met in the fog.

"I believe I met you just last night, Mr. Skelton," I said as we entered the school.

"Last night?" he repeated.

"I don't think you noticed me," I added. "I spoke to you, but you did not reply."

"I'm sorry, sir," the schoolmaster said, "but it must have been someone else. I did not go out yesterday."

How could that be? I suppose I could have mistaken the man's face for someone else's, but how could I mistake his limp? What are the odds that I would meet a man with the same face and the same lameness?

He could tell that I was not convinced. He added hastily, "Even if I had not been preparing the boys for the inspection, I never would have gone out—it was too damp and foggy. I must be careful—I have a very delicate chest."

My uneasiness toward the man increased with every word he uttered. Why would he lie to me about something as simple as this?

"Let's proceed with the examination," I finally muttered.

Somehow, he turned an even paler shade of white before nodding his head in agreement and calling the students up in order.

I soon found that, despite the fact that Mr. Ebenezer Skelton was a horrible liar, he was a wonderful schoolmaster. The boys were uncommonly well taught and showed excellence in attendance and good conduct. At the end of the examination, when he said he hoped I would recommend the Pit End Boys' School for the government grant, I couldn't help but agree. I bid Mr. Skelton farewell before continuing on to the Girls' School, but as I came out from the examination, I found him waiting at the door.

He apologized and asked if he could talk to me for a few minutes about the field where the children played. The small patch of grass in front of the schoolhouse was too small, but around the back, there was half an acre of unused land that would be the perfect solution. He showed me the piece of land in question.

"Whose land is this?" I asked.

"Mr. Wolstenholme's, sir."

"Then why don't you ask him? He gave you the schools. I daresay he may be just as willing to give you this lot for the children to play."

"Mr. Wolstenholme hasn't been over here since his return. It's possible he may leave Pit End without honoring us with a visit. I couldn't take the liberty of writing to him."

"If you don't contact him yourself, then I can't put in my report that the government should offer to purchase some of Mr. Wolstenholme's land for a playground to—"

I stopped and spun around.

"Sir?" The schoolmaster looked concerned.

"I thought there was someone else here. A third person not a moment ago."

"A third person?" Mr. Skelton laughed nervously.

"I saw his shadow on the ground between yours and mine."

The school faced north, and we were standing behind the buildings, our backs to the sun. The place was bare of any trees and open, our shadows sharply defined and stretched out before our feet.

"A shadow?" he faltered. "Impossible."

There was not a bush or a tree within half a mile. There was not a cloud in the sky. There was nothing, absolutely nothing, that could have cast a shadow.

I agreed that it was impossible and that I must have imagined it.

"If you see Mr. Wolstenholme," I continued, trying to keep my voice from shaking. "I encourage you to mention the playground to him. I think it will be a nice improvement for the children."

"Thank you, sir," he said. "But I had hoped that you might use your influence—"

"Look there!" I stopped him. "Do you see it?"

We were now standing closer to the back of the boys' schoolroom. On the wall, illuminated in the full sunlight, our shadows—mine and the schoolmaster's—were projected. And there, too—no longer between his and mine but a little way apart as if the intruder were standing back—there, defined as if cast by limelight on a stage, I distinctly saw for just a moment, that third shadow.

As I cried out, I spun around, and it was gone.

"Did you see it?" I asked.

He shook his head. "I saw nothing," he said faintly. "What was it?" His lips were white. He seemed as if he might faint.

"You must have seen it!" I exclaimed. "It was right there! Where that bit of ivy grows! There must be some boy hiding—it was a boy's shadow, I have no doubt."

"A boy's shadow!" he echoed, looking around in a wild, frightened way. "There is no place for a boy to hide."

"It doesn't matter," I said angrily.

I searched the surrounding area, the schoolmaster followed behind me with his scared face and limp. But it was no use. There wasn't any place big enough to shelter even a rabbit.

"But what was it?" I asked, frustrated.

"An… an illusion?"

He looked like a beaten hound, so frightened.

"But you must have seen it?" I tried again.

"No, sir. Upon my honor, I saw nothing. Nothing at all."

His face revealed his lies. I was certain that he had not only seen the shadow but that he knew more about it than he chose to tell me. I was furious. To be the object of a boyish trick and to be pranked by a schoolmaster and his students was too much. It was an insult to myself and my position.

I don't even remember what I said; I'm sure it was something short and stern. I promptly turned my back on Mr. Skelton and the schools and marched back to the village.

As I neared the bottom of the hill, a carriage drawn by a chestnut brown mare dashed up to the door of The Greyhound, and the next moment I was shaking hands with Philip Wolstenholm of Balliol. As handsome as ever, Wolstenholme was dressed quite dapper and didn't look a day older than when I last saw him at Oxford. He gripped both my hands, declared that I would be his guest for the next three days, and insisted on carrying me off to

Blackwater Chase at once. I argued, telling him that I had two schools to inspect tomorrow ten miles on the other side of Drumley, I had a horse and cart already reserved, and that my room at The Feathers Inn was already made. Wolstenholme just laughed.

"My dear fellow," he said, "you will simply send your horse back to The Feathers, and a couple of telegrams can be sent to the schools. Unforeseen circumstances have forced you to put off those inspections until next week!"

And with this, in his masterful way, he ordered the landlord to send my luggage to the manor, pushed me into his carriage, and off we went to Blackwater Chase.

It was a gloomy old place, standing high surrounded by miles of meadow. An avenue of oak trees, now leafless, led to the house. It looked more like a border fortress than an English country mansion. Wolstenholme took me through the art gallery and reception rooms after we had lunch, and then we walked around the park, and in the evening, we dined at the upper end of a great oak hall decorated with antlers, armor, and antique weapons.

"Now tomorrow," my host said as we sat over our wine in front of a blazing fire. "Tomorrow, if we have decent weather, we shall go shooting on the moors, and on Friday, if I can convince you to stay a day longer, we will drive over to Broomhead and have a run with the Duke's hounds. What?" He laughed at the look on my face. "You don't hunt? My dear fellow, what nonsense! All our parsons hunt in this part of the world. Have you ever been down a coal mine?"

"No."

"Then a new experience awaits you! I'll take you down Carshalton shaft and show you where the gnomes and trolls live."

"Is Carshalton one of your mines?" I asked.

"All these pits are mine," he replied. "I am the king of Hades and rule the underworld as well as the upper. There is coal everywhere beneath these moors. The whole place is honeycombed with shafts. One of our richest seams runs under this house, and there are forty men about a quarter of a mile beneath our feet here every single day. There's another one under the meadow, but heaven knows how far that one goes! My father began working it twenty-five years ago, and we have gone on working it ever since. It shows no sign of failing us any time soon!"

"You must be as rich as a prince with a fairy godmother!"

He just shrugged his shoulders.

"Well," he said lightly, "I am rich enough to do whatever I want (and that is saying quite a lot). But then, to always be spending money—always traveling the world—always acting on the impulse of the moment... is that true happiness? I have been trying it out for the last ten years... would you like to see the results?"

He snatched up a lamp and led the way through a series of unfurnished rooms, each filled with piles of suitcases and all shapes and sizes, labeled with the names of various foreign ports. What did they contain?

Precious marble from Italy and Greece. Priceless paintings by old and modern masters. Antiquities from the Nile, the Tigris, and the Euphrates. Enamels from Persia. Porcelain from China, bronze from Japan, and strange sculptures from Peru. Arms, mosaics, ivories, wood-carvings, skins, tapestries, old Italian cabinets, painted bride chests, terracotta—treasures from all countries, all ages, never even unpacked.

Should he ever open them, arrange them, and enjoy them? Perhaps—if he ever became weary of wandering, if he married, if he built a gallery to hold them. If not, well, he might start a museum. What did it matter? Collecting was like fox hunting: the pleasure was in the pursuit and ended with it.

We sat up late that first night, I can hardly say conversing because Wolstenholme did all the talking while I, willing to be amused, led him to tell me more of his wanderings by land and sea.

So, the time passed in stories of adventure, perilous peaks ascended, of deserts traversed, of unknown ruins explored, of dangerous escapes from icebergs, earthquakes, and storms. When at last he tossed the end of his cigar into the fire and discovered that it was time to go to bed, the clock told us it was in the small hours of the morning.

The next day, according to the schedule, we did some seven hours of shooting on the moors. The next day I was to go down Carshalton shaft before breakfast and, after breakfast, ride over to a place some fifteen miles away called Picts' Camp to see a stone circle and the ruins of a prehistoric fort.

Not used to so much physical activity, I slept heavily after those seven hours with a gun and was slow to wake when Wolstenholme's valet came to my room with a waterproof suit for my descent into Hades.

"Mr. Wolstenholme suggests that you don't take your bath until you get back from the mine," the vassal said as he laid the waterproof suit on the back of a chair as elegantly as if he were laying out my best evening suit. "And you should dress warmly underneath this suit, for it is quite chilly in the mine."

I looked at the suit, reluctant to put it on. The morning was frosty, and the idea of being lowered into the bowels of the earth, cold, hungry, and unwashed, was anything but attractive.

Should I tell him I'd rather not go? I thought, but while I was hesitating, the man vanished, and my opportunity was lost. Grumbling and shivering, I got up, donned the cold and shiny suit, and went downstairs.

I heard a murmur of voices as I entered the breakfast room. Inside, I found about a dozen miners standing near the door and Wolstenholme, looking somewhat serious as he stood with his back to the fire.

"Look here, Frazer!" he said with a short laugh. "Here's a pleasant piece of news for you: the bed of Blackwater Lake has cracked. The water completely disappeared in the night, and the mine is flooded. No Carshalton shaft for you today!"

"Seven foot o' wayter in Jukes's seam, an' eight in th' owd north and south galleries," growled a huge redheaded fellow who seemed to be the spokesman.

"An' it's the Lord's own marcy a' happened o' noighttime, or we'd be dead men," added another.

"That's true, my good man," said Wolstenholme. "It might have drowned you like rats in a trap. So, we may thank our lucky stars. And now, to work with the pumps! Lucky for us, we know what to do and how to do it."

He dismissed the men with a good-natured nod and an order for unlimited ale.

I listened in amazement. The lake had vanished? I couldn't believe it. Wolstenholme assured me that this wasn't the first time this had happened to mines. Rivers had been known to disappear in mining districts, and sometimes, instead of just cracking, the ground would cave in, burying not just houses but entire towns.

"And now," he said lightly, "you may take off that fancy costume. Sadly, I must see to business today. It's not every day that someone loses a lake!"

With breakfast over, we went to the mouth of the pit and watched the men fixing the pumps.

Later on, after the work was well underway, we started off across the park to view the scene of the catastrophe. We marched across the meadow and into the nearby woods. Beyond the tree line, we followed a broad glade that led to the lake. Just as we entered the clearing—Wolstenholme joking about the whole affair—a tall, slender lad with a fishing rod came out from one of the side trails to the right, crossed the clearing, and disappeared into the trees on the opposite side. I recognized him instantly. It was the boy whom I saw the other day, just after meeting the schoolmaster on the road.

"If that boy thinks he's going to fish in your lake," I laughed, "he will be quite disappointed."

"What boy?" Wolstenholme asked, looking back.

"The boy that just passed through here a minute ago."

"In front of us?"

"Yes. You must have seen him."

"I did not."

"You didn't see him? A tall, thin boy in a gray suit with a fishing rod over his shoulder. He disappeared behind those Scotch firs."

Wolstenholme just looked at me with surprise.

"You must be dreaming!" He laughed nervously. "No living thing—not even a rabbit—has crossed our path since we entered the park."

"I am not in the habit of dreaming with my eyes open," I replied quickly.

He laughed and put his arm through mine.

"Eyes or no eyes," he said, "you are under an illusion this time."

An illusion—the very word used by the schoolmaster. What did it mean? Could I no longer rely on my own senses? A thousand thoughts and fears flashed through my mind in a moment. I remembered tales of other cases of visual hallucinations and wondered if I had suddenly become afflicted in the same manner.

"Good Lord!" exclaimed Wolstenholme. "What an odd sight!"

We had emerged from the glade and were looking down at the bed of what had been Blackwater Lake just yesterday.

It was, indeed, an odd sight—an oblong, irregular basin of black slime. Less than a quarter of a mile from where we were standing, a crowd had gathered. All Pit End (except the men working the pumps) seemed to have turned out to stare at the bed of the vanished lake.

Hats were removed, and curtsies were dropped at Wolstenholme's approach. He, meanwhile, came up smiling with a pleasant word for everyone.

"Well," he said, "are you looking for the lake, my friends? You'll have to go down Carshalton shaft to find it! It's an ugly sight!"

"'Tis an ugly soight, squoire," replied a blacksmith in a leather apron. "But thar's summat uglier, mebbe, than the mud, ow'r yonder."

"Something uglier than the mud?" Wolstenholme repeated.

"Wull yo be pleased to stan' this way, squoire, an' look strite across at yon little clump o' reeds. Doan't yo see nothin'?"

"I see a log of rotten timber sticking half in and half out of the mud," Wolstenholme said. "And a particularly long reed, apparently... by Jove! I believe it's a fishing rod!"

"It is a fishin' rod, squoire," the blacksmith said. "An' if yon rotten timber is hidin' an unburied corpse, may I never stroike hammer on anvil agin!"

There was a buzz among the bystanders. Of course, it was an unburied corpse, nobody doubted it. Wolstenholme shielded his eyes from the sun, trying to get a closer look.

"It must come out, whatever it is," he insisted. "Five feet of mud, I believe. There's a sovereign apiece for the first two men who wade through it and bring whatever that object is back to the land."

The blacksmith and another man pulled off their shoes and stockings, rolled up their trousers, and jumped in.

They were over their ankles at the first plunge, and picking the safest route with sticks, went deeper with every step. As they sank, our excitement rose. At the moment, they were visible from only the waist upwards. We could see their chests heaving as each step took more effort than the last. They were still twenty yards from their goal when the mud reached their armpits… a few more feet, and only their heads would remain above the surface!

The crowd was uneasy at this point.

"Call 'em back, for God's sake!" a woman's voice cried out.

But at that very moment, the men reached an incline in the slimy lake bed, emerging waist-high.

As they reached the reeds, they stooped low above the shapeless object, and all eyes were on them. Lifting it from the muddy bed, they hesitated and lay it back down again, apparently deciding to leave it there. As they made their way back to us, the blacksmith remembered the fishing rod and turned back, untangled it from the reeds, and carried it back with him over his shoulder.

We didn't even have to ask them what the object had been—their faces said it all.

It was a body. As they tried to lift it, they realized that it was so advanced in decomposition, they didn't want to risk bringing it to shore. From the slenderness of the form, they concluded that it must be the body of a boy.

"Thar's the poor lad's rod," the blacksmith said as he gently laid it down on the ground.

So far, I have related the events as I witnessed them myself. However, from here on out, I must give my story second-hand as I received it several weeks later in the form of a letter from Philip Wolstenholme.

Blackwater Chase, Dec. 20th, 18—

Dear Frazer,

It's been some time since I promised to write to you, but I didn't want to waste either of our times until I had something definite to tell you. I think we've found out all we'll ever know about the tragedy in the lake. I'll begin at the beginning when you left Blackwater Chase, which was the day after we discovered the body.

Just after you left, a police inspector arrived from Drumley, but nothing could be done until the remains were brought to shore. Believe it or not, it took almost a week to do so. We had to sink a multitude of large stones in order to make a path across the mud. We were finally able to use a small cart to bring the body to shore. It proved to be the body of a boy, perhaps fourteen or fifteen years old.

There was a fracture about three inches long on the back of the skull, clearly fatal. Of course, this might have been an accident, but while we were raising the body to the cart, we found that it was pinned down by a pitchfork whose handle had been cut short to not be seen above the water. No doubt evidence for murder. The boy's face was decomposed beyond recognition, but enough of the hair remained to show that it had been short and sandy. As for the clothing, it was a mere mass of rotten shreds, but after careful inspection, appeared to be a suit of light gray cloth.

A crowd of witnesses came forward at this point—for I am now giving you the facts as they came from the coroner—to prove that about a year ago, Skelton, the schoolmaster had a young boy staying with him whom he called his nephew (a young boy who the old man was not kind to). The lad was described as tall and thin with sandy hair. He always wore a suit of the same color and texture as the shreds discovered on the body in the lake, and he was obsessed with fishing in various ponds and streams whenever he found the time.

One thing led to another. Our Pit End shoemaker identified the boy's boots as being a pair of his own design.

Other witnesses claimed that the nephew and uncle fought often. Finally, Skelton turned himself in, confessed to what he had done, and was sent to Drumley Prison for murder.

And the motive? That's the strangest part of the story! The boy was not Skelton's nephew but his own illegitimate son. The mother was dead, and the boy lived with his grandmother in a remote part of Cumberland. The old woman was poor, and the schoolmaster sent her money for the boy's keep and clothing. He had not seen the boy in years before he sent for him to come over for a visit. Perhaps he was tired of sending money away for the boy. He claims that he was upset to find the boy half-witted, stupid, and poorly raised. The boy acted as if he was five years old. When Skelton enrolled him in the Boys' School, he couldn't teach him anything. He was disobedient, talked of nothing but fishing, and would constantly wander off into the countryside with his rod and line. At first, he didn't like the poor boy, and as time went on, he grew to hate him.

At last, Skelton followed him to where he hid his rod, then across the meadow into the park and up to the lake. Skelton's account of what happened next is nothing short of confusing.

He admits to beating the boy about the head and arms with a heavy stick that he had brought with him for that very purpose but denies that he intended to kill him. When his son fell to the ground and stopped breathing, he finally realized how hard he must have hit the lad. He admits that his first impulse was not of remorse for what he had done but of fear for his own safety. He dragged the body among the reeds by the water's edge and tried to conceal it as well as he could.

That night, when the neighbors were all asleep, he snuck out and took with him a pitchfork, rope, old iron bars, and a knife.

He marched across the moor and entered the park at a turnstile and footpath on the Stoneleigh side, walking about four miles. Using the old rotten boat we had tied at the shore at that time, Skelton hauled the body in and paddled his ghastly burden out into the middle of the lake. Here he weighed the corpse down and pinned it with the pitchfork. He then cut away the handle of the fork, hid the fishing rod among the reeds, and believed (as all murderers believe) that he had gotten away with it. According to the folk of Pit

End, he simply told them that his nephew had gone back to Cumberland, and no one doubted him.

Now, however, he says that he was planning on telling the truth—his dreadful secret had become intolerable. He was haunted by an invisible Presence. That Presence sat with him at the table, followed him on his walks, stood behind him in the schoolroom, and watched him as he slept. He never saw it, but he felt that it was always there. Sometimes he still raves about a shadow on the wall of his cell. The prison guards believe that he is insane.

I have now told you all there is to tell at present. The trial will not take place until spring. In the meantime, I am off to Paris tomorrow, and then in about ten days on to Nice, where you can write me at the Hotel des Empereurs.

Always, dear Frazer.

Yours,

P.W.

P.S.—Since writing the above, I have received a telegram from Drumley to say that Skelton has committed suicide. No details were given. So ends this strange story.

By the way, that was a curious illusion of yours the other day when we were crossing the park. I have thought of it many times. Was it an illusion? That is the question.

Yes, indeed. That is the question. And it is a question that I have not yet been able to answer.

Certain things I undoubtedly saw—with my mind's eye, perhaps—and as I saw them, I have described them. I haven't withheld or added anything. Let those solve the mystery who can. As for myself, all I can do is echo Wolstenholme's question:

Was it an illusion?

Figgy Pudding

Inspired by a Recipe from 1896

Ingredients:
3 oz of beef suet (or vegetable shortening)
½ lb of figs, finely chopped
2 and 1/3 cups of stale breadcrumbs
½ cup of milk
2 eggs
1 cup of sugar
¾ tsp of salt

Directions:
1. Grate the suet/shortening and massage until creamy. Add the figs.
2. Soak breadcrumbs in milk. Add eggs (well beaten), sugar, and salt.
3. Combine mixtures.
4. Pour into a buttered pudding mold.
5. Steam for three hours.

Optional Sauce
Ingredients:
2 eggs*
1 cup of sugar
1 tsp of vanilla or ½ tsp of vanilla and ½ a tsp of brandy

Directions:
1. Beat eggs until they are very light.
2. Add sugar gradually. Continue beating.

3. Flavor with vanilla or vanilla and brandy mixture.

*The FDA does not recommend consuming raw eggs for fear of the risk of salmonella.

Christmas would be incomplete without pudding... especially figgy pudding! Christmas pudding, plum (a name for any kind of dried fruit) pudding, and figgy pudding are all names for the classic steamed cake-like dessert that you know from the Christmas carol, *We Wish You a Merry Christmas*.

It has its origins in 14th Century Britain and has changed (for the better) over the centuries. Initially, it was a way to preserve food and acted as a fasting meal in preparation for the Christmas season. It included beef or mutton mixed with raisins, prunes, wine, and spices. Eventually, grains were added, and this "pudding" was stored in animal intestines until it was eaten months later. By the end of the 16th Century, it went from being savory to sweet. Around this time, the English folk song *We Wish You a Merry Christmas* was born as well, and no doubt poor carolers stood on the doorsteps of the wealthy, requesting some of their figgy pudding.

By the mid-17th Century, figgy pudding was a Christmastime staple until the Puritans banned it in 1647. Luckily, King George I reinstated it as a Christmas pudding.

The pudding as we know it today hasn't changed since Victorian times, but the addition of actual figs is a newer development.

The Kit-Bag

By: Algernon Blackwood
1908

When the words "Not Guilty!" sounded through the crowded courtroom on that dark, cold December afternoon, Arthur Wilbraham—leader of the triumphant defense—showed no particular sign that his defense of John Turk, the murderer, on a plea of insanity, had been successful.

"It's what we expected, I think," Wilbraham muttered without emotion. "And personally, I am glad the case is over."

"I'm glad too," said Mr. Johnson, private secretary to Arthur Wilbraham. He had sat in the court for ten days, watching the face of the man who had carried out one of the most brutal and cold-blooded murders in recent years. No man had ever better deserved the gallows.

The counsel glanced up at his secretary. They were more than employer and employee—they were friends.

"Ah yes," he said with a kind smile. "I remember. You want to get away for Christmas. You're going to skate and ski in the Alps, aren't you? If I were your age, I'd come with you."

Johnson laughed. He was a young man of only twenty-six years but still had the face of a boy.

"I can catch the morning boat," he said. "But that's not the reason I'm glad the trial is over. I'm glad it's over because I've seen the last of that man's dreadful face. It haunted me these last ten days. That white skin with the black hair brushed low over the forehead... I shall never forget. And the description of the dismembered body and how it was crammed and packed with lime into that—"

"Don't dwell on it, my dear fellow," Wilbraham interrupted, looking at his friend curiously. "Don't think about it. Such pictures have a trick of coming back when one least wants them." He paused for a moment. "Now go," he added with a smile, "and enjoy your holiday. Happy Christmas, and don't break your neck skiing."

Johnson shook hands with him and took his leave. As he reached the door, he paused and turned suddenly.

"I knew there was something I wanted to ask you. Would you mind lending me one of your kit-bags? It's too late to get one tonight, and I leave in the morning before the shops are open."

"Of course." Wilbraham nodded. "I'll send Henry over with it to your rooms. You shall have it the moment I get home."

"I promise to take great care of it," Johnson added gratefully, delighted to think that within thirty hours, he would be nearing the brilliant sunshine of the high Alps in winter. The thought of that criminal and the court case was like an evil dream in his mind.

He stopped for supper and went home to Bloomsbury, where he rented the top floor in one of those old, grim houses with large, cold rooms. The floor below his was vacant and unfurnished, and below that were other lodgers whom he did not know. It was a cheerless place, and he looked forward to the change in scenery.

The night was even more cheerless. A cold, sleety rain was driving down with a frigid wind. It howled dismally among the big, gloomy houses, and when he reached his rooms, he could still hear it whistling and howling over the world of black roofs beyond his window.

In the hall, he met his landlady, shielding a candle from the drafts with her hand. "This come by a man from Mr. Wilbr'im's, sir."

She pointed to what must be the kit-bag. Johnson thanked her and took it upstairs with him. "I shall be going abroad in the morning for ten days, Mrs. Monks," he called out as he marched up the stairs. "I'll leave an address for any letters."

"And I hope you 'ave a merry Christmas, sir!" she said in a loud, hoarse voice that suggested spirits. "And better weather than this!" she added.

"I hope so too!" replied her lodger, shuddering a little as the wind went roaring down the street outside.

When he got upstairs, he heard the sleet rapping against the window panes. He put his kettle on to make a cup of hot coffee and then set about packing his kit-bag.

He liked the packing, for it brought the snowy mountains to his mind's eye and made him forget the unpleasant scenes of the past ten days.

Johnson looked to the kit-bag that his friend had lent him. It was a stout canvas bag, sack-shaped, with holes around the neck for the brass bar and padlock. Granted, it was a bit shapeless and not much to look at, but it was deep and wide… there was no need to pack carefully.

He shoved in his waterproof coat, his fur cap and gloves, his skates and climbing boots, his sweaters, snow boots, and earmuffs. On top of these, he piled his woolen shirts and underwear, his thick socks, and knickerbockers. The dress suit came next, in case he was required to dress for dinner at the hotel, and then thinking of the best way to pack his white shirts, he paused for a moment.

That's the worst part about these kit-bags, he mused. *Everything wrinkles so easily.*

It was after ten o'clock. A furious gust of wind rattled the windows as though to hurry him up, and he pitied the poor Londoners whose Christmas would be spent in such a nasty storm while he would be skiing over snowy slopes in bright sunshine and dancing in the evening with rosy-cheeked girls. Ah! That reminded him: he must pack his dancing pumps and evening socks.

He crossed over from his sitting room to the cupboard on the landing, where he kept his linens.

And as he did so, he heard someone coming up the stairs.

He stood still for a moment on the landing, listening. It was Mrs. Monks's step, he thought. She must be coming up with the last of the post. But then the steps paused suddenly, and he heard no more. They were at least two flights down, and after a moment of thought, he came to the conclusion that the footsteps were too heavy to be those of the old landlady. No doubt, they belonged to a lodger, coming home late at night, who had mistaken his floor for their own.

Johnson went into his bedroom and packed his pumps and dress shirts as best as he could.

The kit-bag by this time was two-thirds full and stood upright on its own base like a sack of flour. For the first time, he noticed that it was old and dirty, the canvas faded and worn. It was not a very nice bag to have sent him—certainly not a new one or one that his friend valued. He gave the matter a passing thought and went on with his packing.

Once or twice, however, he caught himself wondering who it could have been wandering down below, for Mrs. Monks had not come up with any letters, and that floor below was empty and unfurnished. From time to time, moreover, he was almost certain he heard a soft tread of someone running across the wooden floorboards—cautiously and as quietly as possible. And as time passed, the footsteps grew louder and closer.

For the first time in his life, Johnson began to feel frightened. As if to emphasize these eerie feelings, an odd thing happened: as he left the bedroom, having finally packed his white shirts, Johnson noticed the top of the kit-bag had fallen over toward him, somehow resembling a human face. The canvas fell into a fold like a nose and a forehead, and the brass rings for the padlock perfectly filled the position of the eyes. A shadow—or was it a stain from years of travel?—looked like hair. It made Johnson jump... for it was so outrageously like the face of John Turk, the murderer.

He laughed and went to the front room, where the lights were brighter.

That horrible case, he thought with a shiver. *I cannot get out of London soon enough.*

The comfort the bright lights of the sitting room brought him only lasted for a moment. Again, he heard the stealthy tread of someone on the stairs, much closer than before.

This time, he stood up and went out to see who it could be creeping about on the upper staircase at so late an hour.

But as soon as he opened his door, the sound ceased, and there was no one on the stairs. Nervously, he tiptoed down the stairs to the floor below and turned on the electric light to make sure that no one was hiding in the empty rooms of the unoccupied suite. There wasn't a piece of furniture large enough to even hide a dog. Then he called over the banister to Mrs. Monks, but there was no answer, and his voice echoed down into the darkness of the house and was lost in the roar of the wind that continued to howl outside. Everyone was in bed and fast asleep—everyone except himself and the owner of this soft and stealthy tread.

Must have been my imagination, he thought. *It was just the wind after all... although... it seemed so real and so close.*

He returned to his rooms as the clock struck midnight. Realizing just how late it was, he quickly finished his coffee and lit another pipe—the last before heading to bed.

It is always difficult to pinpoint the moment when fear begins, especially when its cause is unseen to the human eye. Images flash in the mind's eye, piece by piece, slowly and gradually until those images manifest into a definite emotion and the mind suddenly realizes what has happened. It was at this moment that Johnson recognized with a start that he felt nervous... frightened.

"Nothing more than travel nerves," he said out loud and forced himself to laugh. "Nothing a little mountain air won't cure. Ah!" he added, still talking to himself, "that reminds me—my snow glasses."

As he marched quickly from his bedroom toward the sitting room to fetch his glasses from the cupboard, he saw out of the corner of his eye the distinct outline of a figure standing on the stairs, a few feet from the landing. They were crouched down, with one hand on the banister and their face peered up toward the landing. At that same moment, Johnson heard the sound of a shuffling footstep. The person who had been creeping about below all this time had at last come up to his own floor. Who in the world could it be? And what in the world did he want?

Johnson gasped and stood still. Then, after a few seconds' hesitation, he found enough courage to turn and investigate.

The stairs, he saw to his surprise, were empty... there was no one there. A shiver ran through his body, and the muscles in his legs suddenly grew weak. For several minutes he peered into the shadows at the top of the staircase where he had seen the figure, and then we walked quickly—nearly ran—into the bright light of his sitting room. He hardly passed through the doorway when he heard someone come up the stairs behind him and went swiftly into his bedroom. It was a heavy (but at the same time a stealthy) footstep—no doubt the tread of someone who did not wish to be seen. It was at this precise moment that the nervousness that Johnson had been feeling up until now leaped the boundary line and entered the state of fear. In no time, Johnson's fear threatened to cross the threshold of terror and possibly even pure horror.

"I knew there was someone on the stairs," he muttered to himself, his flesh crawling at the idea of someone hiding in his own home. "And whoever it was has now gone into my bedroom."

His delicate pale face turned pure white, and he hardly knew what to think or do for several minutes. Then he realized that the longer he remained in the sitting room, the more his fear would turn into terror. He boldly crossed the landing and went straight into the other room, where he knew someone was waiting for him.

"Who's there?" he called out loud as he made his way to his room. "Is that you, Mrs. Monks?" He heard his words echo down the empty stairs into the darkness.

"Who's there?" he called again, trying to keep his voice from shaking. "What do you want?"

The curtains swayed ever so slightly, and Johnson's heart skipped a beat. He dashed forward and threw them aside. A window, streaming with sleet and rain, was all that met his gaze. He continued to search the room—the cupboards held nothing but clothes, and under his bed, there was no sign of anyone hiding.

He stepped back into the middle of the room and, as he did so, stumbled over something. Turning in alarm, he saw the kit-bag.

That's odd, he thought. *That's not where I left it.*

A few moments before, it had been on his right, between the bed and the bath. He certainly didn't move it. Curious… very curious indeed.

The wind roared, dashing a wave of sleet against the window before howling over the rooftops of Bloomsbury. A vision of the Channel rose in his mind and brought Johnson back to reality.

"There's no one here. That's quite clear," he exclaimed out loud. Yet as the words left his mouth, he knew perfectly well that they were not true and that he did not believe them himself. He knew someone was hiding close to him, watching his movements, trying to stop him from packing.

He went back to the sitting room, poked the fire into a blaze, and sat down before it to think. He could find explanations for the mysterious footsteps and even the figure on the stairs… but what made him stop and scratch his head was that blasted kit-bag. It had no doubt moved… it had been dragged nearer to the door.

Outwardly, Johnson remained calm, pretending that everything he witnessed had some sort of natural explanation… or perhaps this was all just the delusions of his tired nerves. But in his heart and soul, he knew all along that someone had been hiding downstairs in the empty suite when he came home, that this person had waited for the perfect opportunity to make his way up to the bedroom, and that all he saw and heard afterward, from the kit-bag moving to—well, to the other things this story has to tell—were caused directly by the presence of this mysterious, invisible person.

And it was here, just when he desperately wished to keep his terrified thoughts under control, that the vivid pictures from his days spent in the courtroom came to light and were ingrained in his mind's eye. Haunting memories have a way of coming to life when the mind least desires them—in the silence of the night, as one tosses and turns in bed, during those lonely vigils spent by sick and dying beds. And so now, in the same way, Johnson saw nothing but the ugly face of John Turk, the murderer, glaring at him from every corner of his mind—the white skin, those wicked eyes, and the fringe of black hair hanging low over the forehead.

"This is ridiculous!" he exclaimed, jumping up from his chair. "I must finish my packing and go to bed. I'm exhausted. No doubt, I'll keep seeing and hearing things all night!"

But his face was deadly white despite his brave exclamation. He snatched up his glasses and walked across to the bedroom, humming a cheerful tune as he went—a trifle too loud. The instant he crossed the threshold and stood inside his bedroom, his heart froze, and every hair on his head stood up.

The kit-bag lay in front of him, several feet closer to the door than he had left it, and just over the crumpled top, he saw a pale face slowly sinking down, out of sight. It was as though someone was crouching behind it trying to hide, and at the same moment, Johnson heard a long, drawn-out sigh, hanging in the still air all around him between the gusts of wind outside.

A wave of terror came over him. His legs trembled, and he fought the hysterical impulse to scream. That sigh seemed to be in his very ear, and the air surrounding him still quivered with it. There was no doubt in Johnson's mind… it was a human sigh.

"Who's there?" he was finally able to find his voice, though it came out more like a whisper.

He stepped forward so that he could see all around the kit-bag. Of course, there was no one there, nothing but the faded carpet and the bulging canvas sides. He threw open the mouth of the sack where it had fallen over, and he saw for the first time that around the inside, some six inches from the top, there ran a broad crimson smear. It was an old, faded bloodstain.

Johnson screamed and drew back from the bag as if he had been burned. At the same moment, the kit-bag gave a faint but unmistakable lurch forward toward the door.

Johnson collapsed backward, searching with his hands for something to support himself. The door, farther behind him than he realized, caught him just in time to prevent him from falling and slammed with a resounding bang. At the same moment, his left arm swung out, accidentally shutting off the electric switch, plunging the room into darkness.

It was a most disagreeable predicament, and if Johnson had not kept his wits about him, he might have done all manner of foolish things. Somehow, he managed to pull himself together and groped furiously for the little brass knob to turn the light on again. But the rapid closing of the door had caused the coats hanging on it to swing back and forth, and his fingers became tangled with the sleeves and pockets, so it was some moments before he found the switch. In those few moments of bewilderment and terror, two things happened that sent him deep into the region of genuine horror—he distinctly heard the kit-bag shuffling heavily across the floor, and close in front of his face, he once again heard the sound of someone sighing.

In those few seconds of desperation, as he searched for the light switch, Johnson had time to realize that he dreaded the return of the light and that it might be better for him to stay hidden in the merciful darkness. But this fearful thought barely crossed his mind before he found the brass knob, and the room was flooded with light once more.

His fears had been right, though. It would have been better for him to have stayed in the shelter of the darkness. For there, right before him, bending over the half-packed kit-bag, clear as life in the merciless glare of the electric light, stood the figure of John Turk, the murderer. The man stood not three feet from him—the fringe of black hair hung against the pale forehead—as vivid as Johnson had seen him in the courtroom.

In a flash, Johnson realized what it all meant: the dirty and much-used bag, the smear of crimson within the top, the dreadful stretched condition of the bulging sides. He recalled how the victim's body had been stuffed into a canvas bag, the dismembered pieces stuffed with lime into a bag… this very bag that had been produced as evidence.

As quietly as he could, Johnson groped behind him for the doorknob. But before he could turn it, the very thing he feared most came about, and John Turk lifted his devil's face and looked at him. At the same moment, that heavy sigh rang through the room once more and whispered, "It's my bag, and I want it."

All Johnson remembered was clawing the door open and then falling into a heap upon the landing as he tried frantically to make his way to the sitting room.

He remained unconscious for some time, and it was still dark when he opened his eyes and realized that he was lying on the cold floorboards, stiff and sore. Then the memory of what he had seen rushed back into his mind, and he promptly fainted again. When he woke a second time, the wintry dawn was just beginning to peek through the windows, painting the stairs a cheerless, dismal gray, and he managed to crawl into the sitting room and cover himself with an overcoat in the armchair, where at last he fell asleep.

A great clamor woke him up. He recognized Mrs. Monks's voice, echoing through the apartment right away.

"What? You ain't been to bed, sir? Are you ill, or has something 'appened?" Her voice grew louder as she entered the room. "And there's a gentleman here to see you, though it ain't seven o'clock yet. He says it's urgent."

"I'm all right. Thank you, Mrs. Monks," he stammered. "Who is it?"

"Someone from Mr. Wilbr'im's office, and he says he ought to see you quick before you go away for the holiday. I told him——"

"Show him up, please, at once," said Johnson, whose head was whirling and still filled with dreadful visions of the long night.

Mr. Wilbraham's man came in offering his apologies and explained briefly and quickly that an absurd mistake had been made and that the wrong kit-bag had been sent over the night before.

"Henry somehow got hold of the one that came over from the courtroom, and Mr. Wilbraham only realized it when he saw his own lying in his room and asked why it had not gone to you," the man said. "I'm afraid he must have brought you the one from the murder case instead," the man continued without any emotion on his face. "The one John Turk packed the dead body in. Mr. Wilbraham is quite upset about it, sir, and told me to come over first thing this morning with the right one, as you were leaving by boat."

He pointed to a clean-looking kit-bag on the floor which he had just brought. "I'm to bring the other one back, sir," he added casually.

For a few minutes, Johnson could not find his voice. At last, he pointed in the direction of his bedroom. "Would you be kind enough to unpack it for me? Just empty the things out onto the floor."

The man disappeared into the other room and was gone for only five minutes. Johnson heard the shifting of the bag and the rattle of the skates and boots being unpacked.

"Thank you, Mr. Johnson," the man said, returning with the bag folded over his arm. "Can I do anything more to help you, sir?"

"What is it?" Johnson asked, seeing that the man still had something he wished to say.

The man shuffled and looked mysterious. "Beg pardon, sir, but knowing your interest in the Turk case, I thought you'd like to know what's happened—"

"Yes."

"John Turk killed himself last night with poison, immediately upon his release, and he left a note for Mr. Wilbraham saying he'd be much obliged if they'd have him buried—same as the woman he murdered—in the old kit-bag."

"What time? When did he do it?" Johnson was almost too afraid to ask.

"I believe it was ten o'clock last night."

Meet the Authors

Anna Alice Chapin
(1880-1920)

Anna Alice Chapin was an American author and playwright, publishing her first book when she was only seventeen years old. She wrote novels, short stories, and fairy tales. Her most famous work was the 1904 adaption of the *Babes in Toyland* operetta.

Robert Louis Stevenson
(1850-1894)

Robert Louis Stevenson was a Scottish novelist, poet, and travel writer from Edinburgh. He is best known for *Treasure Island, The Strange Case of Dr. Jekyll and Mr. Hyde,* and *Kidnapped.*

J.H. RIDDELL
(1832-1906)

Known by her penname, J.H. Riddell, Charlotte Riddell was a famous and extremely influential Irish-born author. She wrote over fifty books, novels, and short stories and became part-owner and editor of *St. James's Magazine*, a successful literary journal in London in the 1860s.

THOMAS HAYNES BAYLY
(1797-1839)

Thomas Haynes Bayly was an English poet, songwriter, playwright, and writer. He wrote nearly a dozen songs but is most remembered for *The Mistletoe Bough* (c.1830) and *Long, Long Ago* (1833).

ELIZABETH GASKELL
(1810-1865)

Also referred to as Mrs. Gaskell, Elizabeth Gaskell was an English novelist, biographer, and short story writer. Her book, *The Life of Charlotte Brontë*, published in 1857, was the first biography of Charlotte Brontë. Her writing offers a detailed look at Victorian life, including that of the very poor. Some of her most famous novels are *Cranford, North and South,* and *Wives and Daughters* (all adapted for television by the BBC).

F. MARION CRAWFORD
(1854-1909)

Francis Marion Crawford was an American writer known for his strange and unusual tales. He wrote over fifty novels, plays, and essays and placed many of his stories in Italy. Many of his novels and short stories were turned into films throughout the silent film era.

CATHERINE CROWE
(1790-1872)*

Catherine Crowe was an English novelist specializing in supernatural fiction, plays, and children's stories. She is most famous for her nonfiction work, *The Night-Side of Nature*, the first academic collection of paranormal claims. She is credited by many historians and researchers for laying the groundwork that would lead to the Society for Psychical Research and paranormal investigation as we know it today.

*Some historians say she lived from 1803-1876

E.F. Benson
(1867-1940)

Edward Frederic Benson was an English novelist, biographer, archaeologist, and short story writer. With over sixty novels, over thirty biographies and nonfiction pieces, and dozens of "spook stories," even H.P. Lovecraft was a fan of E.F. Benson. Most notably, his 1906 short story, *The Bus Conductor*, was adapted into a 1961 episode of *The Twilight Zone*.

ADA BUISSON
(1839-1866)

Ada Buisson was a British writer born in Battersea. Having died at just twenty-seven years old, much of her writing has been forgotten. Two years after Ada's death, *The Ghost's Summons* was published in fellow novelist and fellow ghost story writer, Mary Elizabeth Braddon's magazine, *Belgravia*.

John Berwick Harwood
(1828-1899)

John Berwick Harwood was an English writer best known for his ghost stories (usually published as Anonymous). He wrote over twenty novels and several Christmas ghost stories.

Amelia B. Edwards
(1831-1892)

Amelia Ann Blanford Edwards was an English novelist, journalist, and Egyptologist (known as the Godmother of Egyptology). She wrote over a dozen novels, including *Barbara's History* (1864) and *Lord Brackenbury* (1880), as well as several ghost stories.

Algernon Blackwood
(1869-1951)

Algernon Blackwood was an English broadcasting narrator, journalist, novelist, and short story writer, known chiefly for his ghost stories. Many authors have been inspired by Blackwood, including J.R.R. Tolkien and H.P. Lovecraft.

Amanda R. Woomer
(1990-)

Writer, anthropologist, and paranormal researcher, Amanda R. Woomer is a featured writer for the award-winning *Haunted Magazine* and *The Morbid Curious*, as well as the owner of Spook-Eats. She is the author of several books for adults as well as two books in the *Creepy Books for Creepy Kids* series. She is also proud to be the creator of *The Feminine Macabre*. Follow her spooky adventures or purchase books at spookeats.com and on Facebook, Instagram, and Twitter @spookeats.

Printed in Great Britain
by Amazon